SAVAGE
Hunger

SAVAGE SHIFTERS

NEW YORK TIMES and USA TODAY
BESTSELLING AUTHOR

MILLY TAIDEN

Published By

Latin Goddess Press

Winter Springs, FL 32708

http://millytaiden.com

Cover by: Willsin Rowe

Edited by: Tina Winograd

Formatting by: Lia Davis at Glowing Moon Designs

SAVAGE HUNGER

Isaline Primrose doesn't let anyone cut the line at her mom's bakery, no matter how tall or sexy he his. His custom suit, expensive haircut, and deep brown eyes are making her want things. Very dirty things. It's totally fine to look even if he is a bossy jerk. But is it okay to have naked fantasies with the commanding business man?

Beast Harte doesn't do small towns, but Full Moon Bay has something other towns don't: the perfect building for his deceased father's long-time dream. When he meets his mate, life should be perfect. It isn't. Pissing her off was not in his plans, but he wasn't used to taking orders, only giving them. Now he has his work cut out for him.

Isaline sets up some challenges to see if Beast is the right man for her. What neither knows is other players are at work with their own hidden agendas. Beast guarantees two things—he's getting his mate and his building, and he won't let anyone get in his way.

— For my husband. My fire-breathing dragon.

You are my rock. You give me strength. Walking into that room that day and meeting you was the best thing that could have ever happened to me. You've made me whole.

I love you.

ONE

Beast Harte glanced out the glass panel wall of his Fifth Avenue office. Snow fell over Manhattan giving the city a wonderland appeal. Tourists filled the streets. He liked tourists. They brought his hotels lots of business. But it wasn't his hotels that worried him at the moment. It was the delay in his latest project in the town of Full Moon Bay.

A soft knock at his door took his attention from the fat white flakes falling faster every minute.

"Come in," he barked, turning to face whoever was going to annoy him now.

The door opened and his VP of Acquisitions, Fierce Bradford, walked in.

"I have news on project Little Rose."

Little Rose. That's the name his father had given the lot Beast had set his sights on for his newest condo project. His father had started the Harte Corporation buying small buildings and renting out storefronts. Beast had taken it to a new level ten years ago. He focused on luxury hotels and created the Harte Group, combining the construction, leasing, hotels, and other businesses his parents and he owned under one umbrella.

"Tell me you got the renter to sign the contract."

Fierce raised a brow. "We've been back and forth with this for months and you think she'd just sign it because you sent a fruit basket?"

"Uh, yeah?" he growled. "Wasn't that the idea when we sent it? To soften her up?"

Fierce gave a sharp laugh. "You're getting funny in your old age."

Beast snarled, "I'm younger than you."

"Yeah, but not as good looking. Wolves age better than dragons."

Beast scowled. "So what the hell is the news, that she didn't sign? That's not news. That's been our problem for six months now."

"Yeah," Fierce nodded with a slight twitch of

his lips. "But I came up with a great plan. What if we offer to move her bakery out of the building and pay her rent for a year? Heck, we can even give her a new lease at Analai Hills, maybe even rent free for a few years if she goes for that."

"Isn't your pack from Analai Hills?"

Fierce grinned. "That's right. The Silver Tip Pack has an empty storefront we can give her and there should be no problem moving her over."

Beast raised a brow. "If she agrees."

Fierce sighed and sat down. "If. Big if. So, I could personally go there and —"

"No. I'll go."

Fierce's eyes widened. "*You* will?"

"Stop looking at me like that. You know when I want something done, I handle it myself if it's taking too long."

Fierce gave a loud chuckle. "Yeah, you will. I just didn't realize you'd lost patience already."

"It's been six months of trying to nicely get this woman to give me back my property."

"You make it sound like she stole from you. She does pay rent. Early. Every month. And it's not her fault your father made a deal with her back in the day."

He snorted. "Nobody has a lease as good as

3

she does. She knows she won't get anything like that again and is trying to keep her contract intact." He glared at Fierce. "It doesn't matter. I'm getting my building and project Little Rose will be back on track."

"You might scare them with that attitude, which leads me to believe this is not all about the project. You're pissed over something else and I have an idea what," Fierce told him. "Let me guess, Rinelle LeFevre hasn't gotten the picture that you are no longer interested in her and she doesn't know how to take no for an answer?"

Beast growled. "Maybe."

"It was bound to happen. She's a model. She's the one who breaks hearts, not the other way around."

"Too fucking bad. I'm no longer interested in listening to her whine about seeing her photos without makeup in magazines."

Fierce burst into raucous laughter. "Priceless. That chick is so full of herself, I don't know what possessed you to go out with her to begin with."

Beast knew. He'd been courting her father for a land sale and going through her made things easier. Now, he didn't want to spend any time with her and she didn't get the picture. Going to handle the Little Rose deal was easier than wondering when she'd show up at his penthouse trying to get back together with him.

"I'm done waiting around. I'm going to handle this myself."

"Yeah," Fierce chuckled. "You're running from a needy woman. Did you think that maybe she'll still be around when you get back?"

He motioned his friend to get out of his office when his phone rang. "Did you think that maybe she'll have moved on to someone else when I do?"

Fierce got up and headed for the door. "You can hope. Call me if you run into any trouble."

Beast picked up the phone and sighed. "Hello, Mother."

"You can call me mom, son. M-O-M. Try it. Sounds nice. Like you care that I'm calling."

He ran his fingers through his short hair and clenched his jaw. "Mom. How are you?"

"Good, sweetheart. I miss you. When are you coming to visit?" she asked, her tone sugary sweet.

His mother was good at making a dragon feel like a human teenager.

"I'm about to go on a business trip to handle something. I'll try to swing by when I return."

"Try?" His mother gasped. "Try? How about

5

if I had only tried to give birth to you? How about if instead I'd have let you sit in my belly, wanting to be born?"

He rolled his eyes and tried to keep his lips from lifting into a grin. "Mom, I'm going on two hundred years old."

"So?"

"I'm a little old for you to use that line on me."

"I think you need to learn from your sister and get your ass over here at least once a week."

He leaned back in his office chair and turned to look out the window to the continued falling flakes. "You want me to be like Storm?"

"Not like her, but maybe try to visit more often. I miss you, son."

He sighed, hearing his mother's sadness through the line. "I'll see you when I get back. I promise."

"Thank you. I'll make you some stew. I know you love my beef stew."

"I do. I have to go."

"I love you, son. You might have that whole dragon fire in you, but to me, you're always my cute dragonling that needed his momma during his first shift."

He grinned and turned back to his desk. "I love you, too, Mom."

He hung up and picked up the file on the project Little Rose. A few hours and he'd get the contract signed. Nothing and nobody was going to stop this from happening. His condos were going up in the small town of Full Moon Bay.

TWO

Isaline Primrose couldn't believe her eyes. "Is that snow?"

Becky, her assistant at the bakery when her mom wasn't around, nodded. "Yeah. It's a little soon to be snowing, isn't it?"

"You mean because we had that nice warm front and you were wearing spring clothing and now you're back to heavy coats?" Isaline sighed. "I really hoped there would be no more snow."

Becky chuckled and handed her a tray of cupcakes to frost. "You love snow."

Isaline nodded vigorously. "Oh, I do. It's so pretty and stuff, but I just bought new spring dresses and wanted to wear them all before it got cold again."

"Then wear them. Don't worry if it's cold." Becky placed a piece of Isaline's famous chocolate cake on a plate and handed it to a customer. He smiled and winked as he handed her a large bill to pay for the cake.

Isaline piped lemon frosting onto her finger and licked it. She groaned at the taste of the sweetness. "I can't. God, I love cake and frosting, and fuck, if Mom sees me she'll have kittens."

Becky gave the guy his change and turned to face Isaline. "Oh, stop. You've been so good. You've stuck to eating healthier. You've made it your business to exercise more and cut down sweets to only your cheat day."

Isaline shook her head. "Not this week. I've been struggling."

Becky patted her on the shoulder. "I understand. Be kind to yourself, Isa."

She nodded and passed the heavy frosting bag to Becky. It was time for dinner with Zuri and Sage, and she didn't want to be late. With Sage visiting only once a month to give her mom a week with baby Baron, things were crazy.

As if that wasn't bad enough, Zuri stayed deep in her mountain, helping Savage handle his bears and raising little Cammi. She and Zuri never had much together time anymore. Sister dates once a month was all Isa got unless she went to visit them, or they happened to come to town for business.

She slipped on her puffy coat and shoved a fluffy beanie with a big ball on her head. "See you tomorrow, Becky."

"Oh, Isa!" Becky called out when she was about to grab the door handle.

She turned to face Becky with raised brows. "What's up?"

"Do you mind opening tomorrow? I have to take my nephew to the doctor. My sister has an early class at the university and I promised."

"Sure thing. I'll be here. Not like I have a life anyway."

Becky smiled wide. "Patience, grasshopper."

Isaline rolled her eyes. "That's what my dietician says when I tell her I'm still having chocolate dreams. The kind where I am in tub full of chocolate sauce and want it to stop so I don't wake up hungry."

"Yeah, that sounds delicious and rough when you're trying to be good."

Isaline groaned. "Tell me about it. No worries on the schedule. I'll be here, and you can take your time."

Outside the bakery, she cuddled deeper into the fur neckline of her coat and glanced down at the piling inches of snow on the ground. A vacation to some place warm sounded nice. That or somewhere she could do something other than stare at the scale, wondering what else she could do to stop thinking about food. It was a constant dilemma seeing as she loved to eat.

The restaurant was only a ten-minute walk from the bakery, and she knew walking was healthier than moving her car. Besides, she had her snow boots on. She was warm and cozy.

Couples whizzed past her to the movie theater. The latest romantic movie was out, and the poor guys were giving their women sad puppy faces but it wasn't working from the looks of that line.

Isaline licked her lips, glad she'd remembered to put lip balm on as she walked out. It was damn cold. Why the hell had she decided to walk?

The Big Bite was her and her sisters' favorite restaurant. She caught sight of Zuri and Sage the minute she walked in and rushed over. Angel, the owner, came by to greet her and took her coat. Her family had been coming to The Big Bite all her life. The restaurant reminded her of her dad and Sunday dinner out with the family.

"So," she squealed, hugging both her sisters again, no longer covered in a puffy coat. "How are you?"

Sage grinned and tossed newly rainbow-colored locks behind her shoulder. "Good. I have great news."

Zuri yawned and picked up her water and took a sip. "Please forgive me if I fall asleep. I'm really tired."

Isaline and Sage gave each other a knowing smile then stared at Zuri. "Are you pregnant?"

Zuri smiled brightly, her happiness shining on her face. "Yes! It's crazy but we're having another baby."

All their screaming and cheers drew the attention of the adjoining patrons and people clapped at the news.

Isaline's favorite strawberry iced tea was placed in front of her along with a big tray of fresh baked bread at the center of the table.

"We already ordered for you," Sage told her as she picked up the sliced carb.

Isaline nodded quietly, watching both her sisters and noticing the changes they each showed from the last time they saw each other.

Zuri had really come into herself. She was a lot bolder and more outspoken than in the past. She'd grown her hair long and wore it in a French braid, probably easier to maintain.

Sage still had her colorful locks, but there was

a relaxed look about her. Sparks of happiness shone in both their eyes. Isaline's chest tightened and a knot filled her throat. She had been thinking a lot about relationships and it was clear to her why she'd been so withdrawn from the dating scene.

Thinking about what her sisters had, she realized she could never settle for less than the type of love they had found.

"So, what have you been up to?" Sage asked, her blue eyes focused on Isaline. "Mom told us you've been really quiet and she's worried."

Isaline shrugged in her oversized sweater. "Nothing. Why are you looking at me like that?"

"Because," Zuri chimed in, leaning forward on the table. "We were wondering what happened to you and Gavin. The guy you had been seeing recently."

Isaline grinned. Her sisters had been really busy and were totally out of it, because she and Gavin had ended things months ago.

"I won't take offense to neither of you remembering, but we broke up."

Sage smacked her forehead and growled. "That's right. He's the one that lasted only a few dates."

"Right. He was nice and all, but once he told me he got a job in Texas, I felt it was a good thing.

He was a bit strange. He attached way too fast. He even wanted a long-distance relationship. He was fun at first, but then he got so needy. That's not for me. Neither is a long-distance relationship."

"Why not?" Zuri asked. "Long-distance relationships can work."

There was silence the moment their food arrived, and Sage immediately started stabbing her pasta, her lips pursed.

Zuri sipped her water.

Isaline hated tension between them. That's not what their relationship was about. "Guys, please. I hate this. Can we talk about your kids, instead?"

"No," Sage barked. "We can tell you're unhappy, Isa. We can tell something is wrong and we want to help."

Zuri nodded, her eyes full of concern. "We need to help. Mom can tell, too. She's calling us day and night asking if we can set you up with one of the lovely shifters from Feral's pride or Savage's clan."

"Do you want that?" Sage sighed. "We will if that's what you want."

"No." She didn't know what she wanted, but she knew that wasn't the way to go about it. Love would come at its own pace. It just sucked that it

14

was taking so long. She dare not let her sisters know that though she'd dated and been in long-term relationships, she'd only had sex a handful of times, and from those, been fully satisfied even less.

Maybe she was the problem. Wanting something elusive that most women didn't have was probably making it even harder. Her sisters were unique. They were humans with shifter mates and had what could only be described as amazing men. One hundred percent devoted to them. God, if only. Maybe in her next life she'd meet someone like that.

THREE

Isaline shivered the minute she got out of her car the next morning. It was so damn cold. Why did she decide to wear such a flimsy sweater under her coat? The cold seeped through the wool lining and she shivered again. Fuck. She rushed to get the shop open and was ecstatic that the heat was on. The bakery was nice and toasty.

She turned on the ovens and pulled trays out for baking. She also prepped the front areas with the cupcakes that would line the shelves later. She got to work on her chocolate cake while she waited for the bakers that handled the pastries and pies.

The store was quiet, and it allowed her time to think. She was glad she had let her mom talk her into baking her cake more often. As it was, she really had no idea what to do with herself. Her last job had ended when the marketing department for the big box store she'd been working for shut down.

Sure, she handled the social media and other accounts of the bakery, but that was something she could do with her eyes closed. She needed more in her life. A purpose.

After her cakes were in the oven, the other bakers arrived, and she focused on setting up the tables and chairs of the dining area. Coffee was brewed, and machines turned on for espresso, hot chocolate, and tea.

Once she opened the front door to the public, the place was jammed packed in no time. She was serving coffee with muffins, ringing up sales and smiling at each customer that complimented her new sweater.

The bakery was completely full and a line going out the door when a tall mountain of a man showed up in a suit that had to be specially made for him and cut the line.

"Sir," she smiled as sweetly as possible without showing a hint of her aggravation for his starting trouble by cutting the line so early in the morning, "there's a line."

He stared at her with piercing gold eyes, his face blank of expression. "I need to see the owner."

"Yes, well," she handed someone else their bagged order and motioned with her head. "That's the line," she said, her voice taking a hard tone.

"I don't think you understand, I have things to do."

She narrowed her gaze. "Yeah? Well, so do all these people and you're making them late. So get your ass to the back of the line or get out."

"I came to see Mrs. Primrose," he barked as if unused to being argued with. Well, today was his lucky day.

"Look, buddy, it's cold and you're pissing me off," she growled. No matter how good-looking he was, she wasn't going to let him skip people that came in every day. "Get in the line or you're never going to see Mrs. Primrose. Got it?"

His brows flew up. A vein appeared on his left cheek and his lips formed a straight line. Before she had a chance to utter another word, he was gone.

She sighed and glanced at her current customer. "What can I get you today, Mrs. Wilhollow?"

The elderly woman grinned and winked at her. "Don't let him get the best of you. He's clearly not from this town. That attitude tells me he's some kind of boss."

"Yeah? Well, he's not the boss of me."

Mrs. Wilhollow giggled. "Besides, with a face like that, I wouldn't mind letting him skip me." She leaned in and whispered, "Imagine how big he is under that suit."

She laughed at Mrs. Wilhollow's comment and let the minor irritation go. Back to work.

The line was finally dead and she had just made herself a cup of coffee when Big, Tall and Annoying showed up again.

He stared at her with curiosity. Then glanced down at the chocolate cake she'd just served to someone. "I'll take a piece of the chocolate cake and an espresso."

"You can have a seat at any of the open tables. I'll bring your items when ready."

He marched to a corner table facing the front window and sat. She loved that spot. Oftentimes she would sit there and drink coffee and people watch.

She placed two pieces of the cake on a plate and brewed his espresso. Once it was ready, she took it to his table.

He glanced up at her as she walked toward him, the piercing look made her uncomfortable and she had the urge to cover up. It was as if he could see through her clothes to the woman beneath. It was strange, and a small fire started at the pit of her belly. No. There was going to be none of that. He was a rude, obnoxious man, and she would not allow herself to be interested in him at all. Not even a little.

"Thank you," he said, his voice low and rough. The hairs on her arms stood on end. Had it been that sexy when he'd demanded to see her mom? He glanced down at the plate and the corner of his lips turned up. "Two pieces of cake?"

"You look like you need something sweet in your life," she remarked, trying to keep the sarcasm out of her tone. "Don't worry, it's on the house."

She turned to walk away, but he grabbed her arm and she froze in place. Her head snapped to glance at the spot where his hand made contact with her skin. Her heart sped up and she could hear her breathing hitch.

"Please, wait." He let go of her arm, but she was too shocked over how that simple touch had made her body react.

Clearing her throat, she shoved shaky hands into the pockets of her jeans and licked her lips. "Yes?"

"I want to apologize."

"You do?" This was new. Men rarely apologized to her. And definitely not any that looked like him.

"Yes, I realize you had a full shop and were busy. My lack of patience put you on the defense. I'm sorry."

She swallowed hard and nodded. "Thank you."

Another customer showed up and pulled her out of the strange staring contest they had going on. Her heart was beating double time. What the hell was that about? She didn't get a chance to stop thinking about it. The man wouldn't take his eyes off her the entire time she was behind the counter. It was unnerving, and at the same time, it made her blush. Who was this stranger?

FOUR

Beast glanced at the rest of the cake he'd brought back to his suite. Having a hotel two towns over made it easy for him to drive to Full Moon Bay. The cake was the best he'd ever had. In all his years as a dragon, he'd tasted enough sweets to know this cake was special. Whoever made it was truly gifted in the art of baking.

"So," Fierce yelled through the speaker on his desk, "did you get a chance to meet Mrs. Primrose?"

"No."

At first, he'd been annoyed by the human female telling him no. Then, when he'd gotten a good look at her pretty blonde hair and big blue eyes, he'd been physically attracted, but he hadn't expected that the moment his dragon got a scent

MILLY TAIDEN

of her, things would get more difficult. He was being kicked out of the bakery when his dragon was telling him that was the one. The female they'd waited all their lives for. His mate.

"What happened? Did she have a bunch of bodyguards or something?"

"She wasn't at the bakery when I went."

"That sucks, bro. But you need to do something soon if project Little Rose is going to happen on the schedule you proposed. We're losing time."

Fuck. A mate. That's the last thing he needed right now. "I'll go back later and hopefully someone can give me more details."

"How's the bakery? Does it suck, and will it be an easy thing to kick them out?"

He frowned. Kicking the female out of the shop was the last thing on his mind. The idea made his dragon want to burn something. "The place is always packed. And it's got a great set up. I'm not surprised she's said no to us thus far."

"But, come on, it's been there for thirty years. There's got to be something falling apart."

"No. They take good care of it. Pull up anything you have on repairs or requests to get things fixed or changed. I want to see what we've done for the property."

23

"Got it. I'll send it over. Is it as cold there as it is here? Kay won't stop complaining all day."

"Kay is human. She feels the weather more than we do."

"True. She makes sure I know it, too." Fierce laughed.

"I'm fine. It feels no different than the city to me."

"All right, then. I'll get that to you and wish you luck convincing Mrs. Primrose to move her very lucrative bakery to a new location." Fierce snorted. "Seems an unlikely task now."

Beast glanced at the boxed cake and frowned. He didn't even know her name. Oh, he'd tried to get her to give him more than two words of conversation, but she clearly didn't like him. Great. This was new. He wasn't used to females, human or otherwise, rejecting him. In fact, thinking about it, he'd never had that particular problem before. Ever.

Beast hadn't gotten where he was in life with his wealth and world-renowned companies by letting something he wanted slip through his fingers.

A trip back to the bakery was in order. If he was lucky, he'd see his grumpy beauty and speak to Mrs. Primrose at the same time. Ideas swirled in his head about how to handle both women.

Mrs. Primrose would need to be convinced to move her bakery, but that was the least of his worries at the moment. The fact he'd found his mate and she hated his guts was a bigger concern.

His cell phone rang with the distinct sound of his mother's ringtone. He growled but stabbed the answer button.

"Hello, Mother."

"Darling! How are you? How's your business trip going? Are you and Rinelle still an item?" As usual, his mother was much too interested in his personal life. She'd slid the question right in there, hoping he would answer it.

"Sorry, Mother. I had to make sure I could get to Full Moon Bay for a contract negotiation."

"I told you to call me mom, Beasty. You are much too serious in your two hundred years," she chastised. "Is this for the Little Rose site?"

"Yes." He tugged the tie off and unbuttoned his shirt, making himself comfortable so he could shower after the call.

"Your father was particularly fond of that site. When that tenant took on the rental, he'd made some comments about sometimes we have to lower our expectations in order to get the best long-term tenant." She sighed. "Whatever that means."

"Do you know if Dad made any special

amendments for this contract? Anything I should look into?"

"It's possible. I remember going over there with him once. We met the woman and her husband. She was a real looker. Long blonde hair and big blue eyes. A smile that screamed pure innocence. If I didn't know your father was one hundred percent in love with me, I'd have burned her to a crisp."

He snorted at the idea of his mother being jealous over a human. His mother was the most beautiful dragoness he'd ever seen in his life. And she'd never lacked self-esteem. She'd known her mate only had eyes for her.

"Funny. I have to think about this. I'll give you a call when I get back in town."

"You never answered my question about Rinelle, son."

He sighed and laid back on the hotel's bed pillows, getting more comfortable to allow his mother to speak. "I know you're not asking because you want me to be with Rinelle. Say whatever you need to."

"Look, honey, I know it's not my business."

He grinned and shook his head. "You always start with that line."

"Well, it's true. It's not, but I worry about you because you're my son and I love you and want you to be happy. But that little girl doesn't even know what bread looks like."

A hearty chuckle left him at that comment. If nothing else, his mother was always on point. Rinelle was always eating crumbs. He hated that. For once, he'd like to have a meal with someone who wasn't worried about how eating a plate of pasta would make her look.

"Really?" He tried to mask his laughter with a cough.

"Oh, don't give me that. Hell, the last time we saw her at the fundraiser, she turned away dessert. Who in their right mind says no to dessert? Why, that's the best part of dinner. She's got to be crazy to dislike food that much."

"Mother," he sat up, trying to stop the laughter, "she's very healthy and has to watch what she eats. She's been doing it all her life. It's what comes naturally."

"Yeah, I know. But you can be healthy and still eat bread. Good lord, Beasty. Bread is life. How can she not eat it? I mean, there was a point in your childhood where all you wanted to eat was bread and cheese."

He grinned at the memory. "I know. But these are different times."

"Listen, son. I get it. She's pretty and has a good family. But don't settle for someone that's good for business. You need someone that's good for your heart. For your dragon."

"All right, I'm going to bed. It's been a long day."

"That's my cue to leave your fiery ass alone. Have a good night, my love."

"Goodnight, Mom."

"Thank you. Now remember that next time we speak."

The phone line died, and he dialed Mrs. Primrose. The woman was harder to get a hold of than the president. She was always gone and busy, never available for him to see, much less speak to.

"Hello, Mr. Harte. How are you this evening?"

"Good evening, Mrs. Primrose. I went by your shop this morning but managed to only upset your employee by asking for you."

There was a moment of silence before she replied. "Please, Mr. Harte, call me Mirabel. Was my employee rude?"

"No. She was just very good at sending me to the back of the line. Pretty feisty." Where had that come from? Beast knew the blonde beauty had sass and that intrigued him. Women didn't speak to him with any kind of authority.

Mirabel laughed at his words. "That had to be Isaline. She's definitely feisty."

"Isaline?"

"She should have been the one to open the bakery this morning. Curvy beauty. Blonde hair and blue eyes?"

"Yes. Beauty is accurate."

"Really, Mr. Harte. Sounds like Isa made an impression on you." Mirabel's voice was full of humor. "Too bad I wasn't around to make sure you got a chance to meet her."

He cleared his throat, thinking of Isaline's frown. "I need to speak to you about the building, Mrs. Primrose, Mirabel. I need that location."

"How about we discuss it over dinner? Join me and my family and we'll talk about what you're proposing."

He didn't want to go to her home and ask her to give up the location she'd had for almost thirty years. He had a good offer, so that made him feel better, but still. For all he knew, her family could be totally against the move and it would be awkward and uncomfortable.

"When?" He wasn't going to lose that building due to some silly emotional attachment Mirabel or her family might have.

"Sunday night. I am actually very busy this

week, Mr. Harte. You'll have to work with my schedule."

He clenched his jaw. Beast had never worked on anyone's schedule but his own. Still, he had to suck it up and make himself wait until Mirabel had time or he'd never get her to change her mind.

"Sounds good. I'll see you Sunday."

"In the meantime, Mr. Harte, please feel free to visit the bakery and have more of our delicious chocolate cake. It's our biggest seller."

"I already had some. And I can see why."

"Goodnight, Mr. Harte. I think this trip will be very interesting for you." Her laughter tinkled in his ear, "Very interesting indeed."

FIVE

Isaline stared at the card that had been delivered with two dozen pink roses. It had to be wrong.

"Oh, Isa!" her mother squealed. "Those are just beautiful." She raised her brows, her eyes twinkling with curiosity. "Looks like you've been busy. And here I thought you weren't dating anyone."

"I...wasn't. These are from Gavin."

Her mother gasped. "Gavin, the guy that moved and you were totally *not* devastated he left, Gavin?"

"Yes, Mom. That Gavin. He's moving back. For me."

"What?"

She sat down at the dining room table and

tried to think about how she felt. Things with Gavin had been so strange. His move had been a good thing for her. It had allowed her to realize dating him wasn't going anywhere. But this...his note. No man had ever quit his job and returned for her. That had to mean something, no?

"You look so confused, darling." Her mom sighed. "Let me make tea and we can chat."

"I already made tea. I had just turned the kettle off when the doorbell rang."

"Okay. I'll get it." It was a few moments before she was back with a tray with tea and mini scones and pastries. She poured Isa a cup and then one for herself before sitting. "So, why do you look so sad that Gavin sent you flowers?"

"It's just...I don't know, Mom. Gavin and I were never all that special. We went on four dates. Who moves for someone they went out with four times?"

"How was the sex?"

"Mom!" She gaped at her mom who was adding sugar to her tea like she'd said nothing wrong.

Her mom raised her brows and stirred her tea. "That bad, huh?"

Heat crowded her cheeks. God.

"We never got around to having sex. I just

didn't feel that kind of chemistry for him. Besides, not everything is about sex," she fired back.

"True. But that's the start. If your sex life sucks, then the rest better be fucking spectacular or what's the point of even calling it a relationship?"

And that was her problem. Nothing had been spectacular. Nothing had been out of this world. His constant calling and showing up at the bakery had started to bug her, so when he mentioned moving, she'd sighed in relief that she wouldn't have to be mean about breaking things off. He'd asked about long distance, but she'd suggested he find someone new. So why had Gavin come back for her?

"Okay. I just don't understand why he'd leave his job to come back to be with me. I just don't get it. We were casual at best. I mean, it's been almost four months since he left. I'm confused. Four dates, Mom."

She sipped on her tea and sighed. The sweet berry flavors along with lavender helped soothe her frustrations.

"Don't be confused. He might think you want more than you do. You've had some time apart. What do you feel for Gavin?"

Nothing. Gavin had been a great friend who also volunteered. When they worked together, he'd been fun, and things had never been complicated. They'd had a good time, which was why she'd finally agreed to go on a date with him, but that had been a mistake. His move had been a lifesaver. It allowed them to remain friends without an awkward breakup. But now he wanted to resume things and she didn't see that happening.

"I guess I'll just have to speak to him," she told her mom. "I'm not interested in dating him. He was way too clingy. I want a relationship that will bring me more."

"Speaking of more," her mother stared at her over the rim of her tea cup, "how was the bakery today?"

She frowned. "Why? What did you hear?"

"I heard a tall, handsome man showed and riled you up."

She rolled her eyes. "People in this town gossip too much."

"So you're saying he wasn't handsome?"

She licked her bottom lip. "I never said that."

Her mom laughed. "Then what are you saying?"

"That people in this town talk too much."

"Oh, stop." Her mother refilled her tea cup. "Tell me about the annoying stranger."

"Mom, he walked in and expected me to stop serving customer because he is whoever he is. I don't care how rich the guy is, there was a line and he wasn't going to skip."

Her mother giggled harder. "You said that to him?"

"Sort of. I told him there was a line and he had to get to the back and no skipping."

"It's not like you to let something bother you this long. Is it still annoying you?"

"I guess it was just how entitled he seemed. Like he was the only person whose needs mattered. I almost slapped him with a slice of cake."

Her mother gasped. "You've never lost your cool like that."

"Yeah, well, he just ticked me off. He was too sexy for his own good. Anyway, he apologized after."

"He did? So then you're over that?"

She shrugged. "I guess. I mean, it's not like I have to deal with the guy again."

SIX

Isaline popped out of the kitchens to place a chocolate cake in the display. She almost tripped over her own feet when she saw Mr. Sexy sitting at one of the tables, drinking coffee and having a piece of her cake.

Why did she have to feel all nervous just looking at him? He wasn't her type. The way he carried himself and how everyone moved out of his way told her he wasn't her type of man. This guy was used to ordering people around. Isaline wasn't a fan of that.

"Look who's here," Becky whispered. "I heard he was here yesterday, too. Mrs. Wilhollow was very particular about describing him when she showed up earlier. She got him down to his expensive haircut and that fallen angel face that could be the stuff of wet dreams."

Isaline frowned hard. She didn't like the idea of other women fantasizing about the sexy stranger. Really? What in the world was wrong with her? Her mind had been busy all night conjuring possible scenarios where she'd see him again. This was not one of them.

"What's he doing here?"

Becky opened her eyes wide and blinked. "He's been waiting for you."

The air in her lungs evaporated and she choked trying to catch her breath. "What? Me?"

Becky nodded. Her lips curved into a smile. "Yeah. You. I was waiting for you to be done back there so you could talk to him."

She tore off the apron and smoothed her sweater over her black leggings. Today was not a good hair day. She'd worn her blonde hair up in a messy bun. She hoped she didn't look like a twelve-year-old.

Nope. She wouldn't care what he thought. Yeah, right. Her hands were already sweating and the thought of his eyes roaming over her like a decadent piece of chocolate gave her goose bumps. Men didn't have that effect on her. Of course, it would be some random stranger from the city that would mess with her hormones and make her feel like a gawky teenager.

"Stop procrastinating," Becky chastised. "Go

see what he wants. I've got bets with Mrs. Wilhollow on him wanting to ask you out or him wanting to hire you to bake for him."

She huffed out a growl, curled her hands into fists, and started to walk over to the table Mr. Sexy had set up with his laptop and turned into his office. She had barely taken two steps before he glanced up and stared at her marching toward him. No pressure. None at all. His gaze bore into hers as she closed the distance between them. God. If she survived this man staring at her, she should win a prize. He really was hell on her nervous system.

"Hi. Becky said you wanted to see me?"

"Isaline?"

She nodded. "Yes, Mr…"

"Beast. Harte."

She raised her brows in surprise. "Your name is Beast? Like *Beauty and the Beast*?"

A slow grin spread over his lips and her breath caught in her throat. God. The man was devastatingly gorgeous. Not even because of the suit or the expensive haircut. He had that rough and rugged look that no suit could hide. She'd bet her entire month's salary he really was a beast in the sheets.

"Yeah. My father said after I was born, I roared like a beast when it came feeding time, so he chose my name. Much to my mother's dismay."

She grinned. "I can imagine. It's a great name. I'm sure nobody messes with you."

His eyes flashed a bright gold. "People don't mess with me, but it has nothing to do with my name."

No. She knew that glow well enough. He was a shifter. The fact he was as big as her brothers-in-law and just as deadly sparked excitement inside her. Death wish. That should be her middle name. Seriously, she was getting hot and bothered because a shifter that was hotter than the sun was staring at her like she was his midday snack. Boy, she'd love to let him nibble on her. "What can I do for you, Mr. Harte?"

"Beast. Please, call me Beast," he said the words in a gravelly voice that made her palms sweat.

She licked her lips. "Beast. What can I do for you?"

"Are you very busy?"

"Not really. Do you need help with something?" She'd stop fantasizing about him and focus on being a humanitarian and help the man out. And then go back to fantasizing about him naked. She wondered if he had any tattoos under all that expensive material.

"I'm not from around here. Would you mind showing me around?"

She cocked her head. "You mean like a guide or a date?"

His perfectly white teeth appeared with his wide smile. Lord have mercy, he was smiling. She almost fanned her face then and there. That smile, and those eyes on her, feeding every dirty thought she had was bad for business. Or at least bad for her to keep her panties on.

"I was hoping if I didn't call it a date, you'd be more willing to agree."

"So you want to go on a non-date with me? And what exactly do you want me to show you? This is a small town. We don't have much to do. Well, we have some stuff, but I don't know if a city person like you would enjoy it. Some of my favorite parts of town are unique to Full Moon Bay."

"I'd offer to take you to dinner, but I'm afraid you'll refuse, so how about you show me around and then we can grab a bite somewhere you like?"

She should say no. This man was way out of her league. But the word no was not coming out of her mouth. "Take your clothes off" were the words she had to fight to keep behind her teeth. Clearly, she had a pervert living inside. "Okay. If you don't mind waiting a few minutes, I'm going to get my bag and we can go."

Becky followed her into the kitchen. "Where are you going?"

"I'm showing him around town," she said, slipping on her wool coat and twining her scarf around her neck. "Wish me luck that I can keep my hands to myself."

Becky snorted. "You're the last person I'd believe would throw herself at a man."

"This guy has something that's making my hormones crazy. I want to tell him to leave and I want to tear at his clothes. It's driving me bananas!"

"I'll say. You've never sounded so frustrated. When was the last time you got laid?"

"God," she groaned. "Not you, too! You're turning into my mother."

"She's a good woman and knows what she's talking about. Maybe this sexy city man will be the meal ticket for your hungry girl bits."

"Oh, ew, Becky!" She made a face. "You make it sound so weird."

"It'd be weirder if you didn't find him attractive. He's hot enough to melt the snow falling outside that window."

Isaline rolled her eyes and chuckled. "You need more lessons with your poetry. He's a sexy man. Big deal. I'll control myself and show him around. Besides, I bet he is just trying to be polite to get me to forgive him for being a jerk yesterday."

Becky raised her brows. "Yeah, right. Girl, he's been looking at you like he wants to make your clothes disappear. If he were Superman, you'd be running around naked."

SEVEN

Isa smiled at the idea of the big, sexy man in tights. "If he was Superman, I'd be looking to find out if the super extends to all areas."

"This is better, Isa. He's a shifter. I bet he's got a killer dick."

A loud giggle left her lips. "You do realize that doesn't sound sexy at all. I'm not trying to get fucked to death."

"Just go with me here. Get him naked. I bet you'll be happy with what you find."

Picking up her cross-body bag, she shook her head. "I'm going to show the sexy stranger around and I will not be getting him naked, you pervert!"

"Don't go to the shelter this time."

Isaline smiled wickedly. "Yes. I may. I think

it would be nice for Beast to feed the homeless, too."

Becky gasped. "You are so evil. That guy is gonna get that gorgeous suit dirty in there."

She shrugged and slipped the bag over her head. "Oh well. He'll survive."

"Evil. Pure evil!" Becky yelled as she walked out.

Beast was outside, waiting next to a luxury car. He opened the door for her and she had to admit it was sweet that he did.

She gave him directions to the shelter she went to every Tuesday. She'd already sent one of the bakers over with several of her cakes to be cut up for dessert.

"So, what is Mercy's House?" Beast asked as they drove down Main Street.

"It's a shelter for the homeless." She watched him for a reaction, but he had an amazing poker face.

"What do you do there?"

She leaned back into the warm leather chair. Leather heated under her butt. She couldn't believe she was in a car that had heated seats. Her Jeep used to belong to her mother before she and her sisters had bought Mirabel a new car and Isa had taken over the old one.

"Feed the homeless."

"Are there many homeless in this small town?"

She shrugged. "They come from neighboring towns. This is the only homeless shelter within thirty miles. A lot of them just need a hot meal."

There was silence the rest of the way. Once they arrived, she watched him remove his tie and suit jacket. When they entered Mercy's House, he rolled up his sleeves and turned to her.

"What do you need me to do?"

"Isaline!" her mother called out. "Who's your guest?"

"Mom, this is Beast Harte. Beast, this is my mom—"

"Honey, don't worry about introductions, we're swamped. Beast," her mom interrupted, "come with me. I have something I need your help with."

She watched her mother walk away, pulling Beast by the arm and chatting animatedly with him.

"Who is that?" Zuri asked, coming up behind her.

"What are you doing here?" She hugged her sister and studied her face to make sure Zuri wasn't overdoing it.

"Mom told me she'd be here, and I wanted to come and help. Savage dropped me off and will be back to get me in a bit. He wanted to get me out of the house since Poppy was taking Savannah so I had a few hours."

"Shouldn't you be resting?" she asked, putting on an apron and hairnet and heading out to the food line.

Zuri did the same but shook her head. "Nah, I feel pretty good today. Not as tired. So I need to take advantage and do things before all I want to do is hibernate." Zuri glanced at the other side of the room where their mother had Beast moving heavy boxes full of canned goods. "You didn't answer my question. Who's the sexy beast?"

Isaline burst into giggles. "His name is Beast."

Zuri opened her eyes wide. "You're kidding! And I thought Savage was a weird name. What is it with shifters and these growly names?"

"You're right. The name alone gives away the fact he's a shifter."

"That and his scent. Dragon."

Isaline gasped, eyes wide and jaw hanging. "His scent? Oh my god. You can scent he's a dragon? Wait, dragon? He's a dragon!"

Zuri grinned. "Yeah. He's a dragon. And yes, I can scent it. Only while pregnant it seems. I never took to the shift, and neither did Sage, but it seems like when I'm pregnant, I have some of their abilities thanks to the baby."

"Wow. That's so cool. Can you tell anything else?" She wanted to know so much more about Beast. He had that quiet, standoffish demeanor but she knew he was interested in her.

"I can tell he wants to get you naked," Zuri scrunched her nose. "You know, that's one I didn't need to scent."

"What do you mean he wants to get me naked?" God, what if he did want to get her naked? Should she let him? She sure as hell had been debating with keeping her thoughts out of the gutter, not that it had been working. But damn, she'd been trying.

Him naked had been the only thing on her mind since last night. She peeked to where he stood listening to her mother give him orders. He was watching her with his face clear of all emotion. Her heart thudded hard in her chest. That look gave her goose bumps. It was full of pure possession.

"Oh, honey," Zuri curled an arm around her shoulder. "You want him. He wants you. What's the problem? I can tell there's an issue even without the fear coming off you in waves."

"He's out of my league. Look at him, Zuri. He

looks like he walked off the cover of GQ magazine. I've never even looked at a man that hot. My goodness. One look from him and my knees are ready to buckle. I can't handle that kind of good looking. I've dated nice guys, but they've never been that smoking hot. It is intimidating."

"Let me tell you something about him. He might be dressed like the epitome of professional, controlled human male that is all about material things, maybe even all about making money and being in the highest of social circles, but he's a shifter. At the end of the day, that man is ruled by his basic desires.

"The need to find a mate and to love her for the rest of his life. The need to breed and continue his line. He might be a billionaire with expensive tastes and fantastic toys, but he is still a shifter. One who will do anything for the woman he loves." Zuri met her gaze and gripped her shoulders. "If you're that mate, there will never be another woman for him. You're his kryptonite. His weakness and his strength."

His kryptonite? But was he her Superman? "But how do I know? I mean, he's a man. He could be interested in me for a little while. I refuse to get into another dead-end relationship. I need to find a forever love. I want that all-consuming love you and Sage have. I won't settle for anything less."

Zuri smiled and nodded. The understanding in her eyes made Isaline feel less silly for her desire to find a happily ever after. "He may or may not be. But like everything in life, you won't know unless you give it a chance."

The line formed to feed those in the shelter and things were super busy for the next hour. She barely got a chance to glance around to see where Beast had gone, but when she saw him sitting at a table talking to Christian Paulos and his dad, Ike, she wondered what was being discussed.

Ike had lost his job when a large manufacturing company closed down. Living paycheck to paycheck had been hard enough, the job loss had left the father and son out on the street. They were living in the shelter until Ike found a job. It was one of the things Isaline had been helping him with. Looking for jobs and sending out his resume.

"He's the one," her mother said beside her.

EIGHT

"Who? What?" Isa frowned, looking around. "Who's the one?"

"Beast. He's the one that owns our building and has been trying to get me to move the bakery into another of his locations."

Isaline gasped and swiftly turned to face her mother. "I'm such a moron. Of course, he is. He's the owner of The Harte Group." She swallowed at the dryness in her throat. The knowledge that he was in town to push her mother into a decision she didn't want fell like a ton of bricks in her stomach.

"He doesn't understand how close we all are in Full Moon Bay. He's from New York City. It's a dog eat dog world out there. Nobody knows anyone and there's too many people to have a small-town feel." She took a drink from a water bottle and sighed. "I'm not moving the bakery."

"Do you know what he wants to do with the building?"

Her mom gave a sad sigh. "He wants to tear it down and build a new hotel in that same area. It's perfect for him. The traffic is great and now that we have a new hockey stadium opening, the area is becoming more popular for people to visit."

"But we're still such a small town. I mean, we don't have a lot of the sights bigger towns do."

"Honey, city folk like the country. They like the small town feel and coming to see our dairy farms. We've gotten big enough, we'll have our first town fair next year. Trust me, that will only bring in more visitors."

She worried her lip and took off the gloves she'd been serving food with. "That's all great, but you shouldn't have to move. He can find other locations to build his new hotel."

Her mom nodded. "I don't think he knows what his father and I had arranged."

"When are you going to tell me about the super-secret arrangement, anyway?"

"One of these days." She patted her cheek. "Go get your dragon, darling. He's been amazing, but it's time to feed him. Besides, he's been staring this way hard. I know he's dying to be closer to you."

She shouldn't allow her mother's words to get her excited, but she couldn't help it. She walked over to where he stood as Ike and Christian walked away and smiled at him. "Thanks for your help. Let's get some food."

She took his hand and led him back to the kitchen area where she kissed her mother and sister and they put their coats on to get into his car.

"Where to now?" he asked.

"Do you like fish and chips?"

"The British version of fish and chips?"

"Is there another?" She laughed. "Yeah. I went to London a few years back with Zuri and Sage as a birthday gift to ourselves and I fell in love with pub food."

She gave him directions and sat back, allowing the warm seat to relax her back.

"You're telling me there's a pub around here?" Disbelief sounded in his voice.

She met his gaze and nodded. "Yes. Believe it or not, our town librarian has family from England. One of her cousins came to visit, fell in love with Full Moon Bay and decided to move his entire family and open an English pub. His family has a cute little log cabin by the river."

"Wow. And the food?"

She groaned. "Delicious. The sticky toffee pudding is so good, you can lick the plate. The fish and chips with mushy peas is delicious. The fish is fresh, flaky, and the crunchy batter makes you want to order seconds. The fat fries are my favorites."

"What else is on the menu that you like?"

She giggled. "Um, everything. I swear I've eaten everything on their menu. The Scotch egg, the Yorkshire pudding, which let me tell you Zuri and Sage got a laugh when I was expecting pudding the first time I ordered it only to encounter a yummy airy soufflé-type bread. I call it bread but really it's not."

"No bangers and mash?"

"Oh yes," she sighed. "I love those. And the meat pies and beef pasties, too. Ugh, as you can see, I can talk about food all day. Mom says I have a deep connection with my taste buds." She laughed. "Thankfully, I started going to a nutritionist, so I learned how to not diet and still eat moderately without binging. I'm a work in progress."

"We all are," he said and covered her hand with his, squeezing hers in his grasp.

She sat up, her heart beating twice as fast. "I think I talked the pub owner's wife into starting an afternoon tea in one of their rooms. We've been bugging her about that for a while."

"You like afternoon tea?" he asked, sounding surprised. "Not a coffee person?"

"I love coffee, don't get me wrong. But being in London and having afternoon tea with scones and biscuits made the day feel extra special. Mom says she's going to buy me a fine china tea set when I get married so I can do my own afternoon tea. Until then, I get to use her set that my grandmother gave her. We do afternoon tea a lot at home. It's something we've adapted since coming back from that trip. Mom loves the idea."

"Your mother is a very lively woman."

She stared at him for a moment. "She is. She's very dedicated."

They arrived at the pub painted in dark green on the outside and trimmed with gold.

"The Prince George?" he asked with a grin as they got out of the car.

She laughed and entered while he held the door. "Hey, they wanted to make sure everyone knew where they were from. Wait till you get inside. It's like being at a royal wax museum."

Inside the pub, they were greeted by Richard, the owner, and his wife, Elizabeth. They were taken to a private booth, but only Beast got a menu.

They gave their drink orders, and once the waitress had left, he glanced at her curiously. "Why was I the only one to get a menu?"

Fire crowded her cheeks and she knew she was blushing fiercely. "I have eaten everything they have here in the past two years. They already know I have my favorites."

He put his menu down and stared at her intently. "Okay. You order for both of us then."

"Are you sure? What if you don't like what I get?"

His gaze never wavered from hers. "I trust you. I'll eat whatever you give me."

Oh, boy. That was a whole other can of worms. She wanted to fan herself again, but it would make it obvious he was making her think all kinds of inappropriate things instead of deciding what to eat. When the waitress returned with their drinks, she got them both the fish and chips.

"I promise you'll love it."

He glanced out the window. "It's snowing again."

"Yeah. It should be for the next few days on and off."

He stared outside, his attention on the falling flakes. "It's much prettier to watch it fall here."

"Why's that?"

He looked at her with that quiet ownership. "Perfect company."

NINE

Isaline bit her lip. God. He was good. He didn't even try to sound romantic and yet he managed to say such lovely things.

"I bet snow is beautiful in New York City. Especially from one of those high-rise buildings or even from a cabin on top of a mountain like where my sister lives."

"Snow falling is beautiful there. Have you seen snow falling atop a mountain cabin?"

She shook her head. "Maybe next winter. I'd like to go up to my sister and her husband's ski lodge and check it out. I'm not into skiing. I'm into hot chocolate by the fire and watching the flakes fall."

"When was the last time you went anywhere?"

She frowned, thinking about his question. Their food arrived, and she was still thinking.

"I guess that London trip was my last real vacation. I haven't really traveled much since. My sisters traveled with their work, but I'm more of a homebody."

"It sounds like you like to travel."

She nodded as she ate. "I do. I'd love to see the world and explore new places, but the opportunity hasn't presented itself. What about you? What do you like to do?"

"According to my mother, my sole purpose in life is to make hers difficult. I disagree. I enjoy traveling as well, but not in the same way you might."

She raised her brows. "What way do you like to travel?"

His eyes flashed gold. "I like to shift, let my dragon roam the skies and spend hours flying."

A swift grin filled her lips. "I should've known. Nature calls to you. Flying is like breathing, isn't it?"

"Yes. I haven't done much flying recently. I've been cooped up in my office in New York trying to work out a deal."

Shit. Was he actually going to talk to her about the contract with her mother and what he was trying to do? "Must be an important deal if you've stopped flying for it."

"I have this idea. Actually, my father had it. He told me the perfect place for the Little Rose Hotel would be this particular lot and I want to make his dream a reality. I'm doing everything I can to get it."

"Oh. It's your dad's idea you're trying to make a reality? Where is he?"

"He died several years ago of an irregular heart condition not even his dragon could fix."

"I'm so sorry," she said, squeezing his hand on the table. "I lost my dad a long time ago. I remember it like it was yesterday still. It never gets easier."

They sat there quietly, sharing a grieving moment before they were interrupted by the waitress bringing their dessert.

"I have to admit," he started. "This is one of the best pubs I've been to on any side of the world."

She laughed and ate her dessert. "The sticky toffee pudding is amazing. I told you."

"As I said, I trust you."

Those words surprised her. He didn't sound like he was being funny or joking. There was no humor in his features. He was serious. He trusted her, and he didn't even know her.

After they ate, he drove her back to the bakery and she turned in her seat to look at him. "Thank you for today."

"Thank you, Isaline. Spending time with you was much better than closing any deal I could have done."

There he went again, being all sweet and romantic without even trying. The nerve.

"Do you want to see more of the town or are you bored out of your mind being in small town nowhere?"

He leaned forward, his body suddenly larger than the space they had in the car. His warmth caressed her face. She wanted oh, so badly, to run her fingers over his face and trace the serious lines there. He should be on a painting or on a bust with that intense look.

"I've never been a fan of small towns, but this one has someone that fascinates me, and is therefore very interesting to me."

He was talking about her. She fascinated him? No. No. No. He was the tall, sexy one with those dreamy eyes and that smile that made her think of hot nights and silky sheets.

This man, he was the one that made her palms sweat. She swallowed hard and leaned a tiny bit closer to him. "You might be out of your depth here, Beast."

A slick grin took hold of his face. "Maybe, but I don't wait around for what I want."

"Oh?"

He raised a hand and cupped her cheek, gliding his thumb over her bottom lip. "No. I see. I want. I take. I'm not going to change how I do things now."

He closed the distance between them and kissed her. It was slow and deep, full of promise and hunger.

Before she got a chance to moan into the sudden invasion, he pulled back, his eyes flaming liquid gold. Fucking hell! She'd shoot him for teasing her. Didn't he know not to mess with a woman who could handle a gun?

"I know you're unsure about me, but that won't last long."

She blinked. "I-what?"

"When you're sure, you'll be mine. No questions. No excuses. You'll come to me and I will show you how much you can trust me."

"I should go," she said, turning to open the door. His hand on her wrist stopped her.

"I'd like to do this again."

She gave a quick nod and licked her lips.

"Tomorrow. Noon-ish for lunch."

He stared at her mouth and nodded. She left the car feeling vulnerable and confused, but also excited and hopeful. Her world had just taken a quick shake and there was no way things were going back to what they used to be.

TEN

Beast parked his car on the street outside the bakery. Sure, he'd driven through small towns before, but he'd never had a reason to stop. Now that he had to be here, he wondered why people were so taken with them. He'd rather be in a big city any day. His research had shown that most small towns more often than not had nothing to offer.

All his friends and business acquaintances lived in the city. And now he was forced to stay here until Mirabel decided to sign his papers. Still, that gave him a chance to convince Isaline to come back to the city with him. Her beauty in this little town was being wasted. He wanted her with him.

He glanced at his watch—9:45 a.m. Ten o'clock was really early for meeting someone for a lunch date in his opinion. Things in the city were always busy. Especially in New York City. It's the city that never sleeps. But this was rural America. They did things differently in places like this. So far, he'd noticed a few people were up super early and that the bakery was packed from the moment it opened.

Straightening his tie, he glanced into the rearview mirror. He made a note that he would need to shave later, even though he had the previous night. How dragons could be so hairy in human form when their animal was all scales baffled him.

Movement seen in the corner of his eye brought up his defenses. He whipped around toward the window and Isaline jumped back, slapping a hand over her heart.

He exhaled and hopped out of the car, ready to go around and open her door. She looked adorable all bundled up. Sort of like a snow bunny he'd like to slowly unwrap to see what lie underneath.

"Good morning," he said, trying to play it cool while he struggled to control his animal. All he'd ever wanted from the first glance into her sexy blue eyes was to claim her and it got harder and harder to control his instinct to do that. Her questioning expression worried him.

"Hi. You're a little early."

He shrugged. "I had nothing else to do and hoped you'd be available."

She nodded, a smile playing her lips. "I see. But you're like…more than a little early. You gave yourself plenty of time seeing that we're meeting for lunch in over an hour from now."

"An hour?" he replied, confused. He knew he'd been distracted by her lips when she'd told him the time, but he had great memory. "Ten a.m., right?"

Isa smiled. "I recall the time set at around noon."

"What?" he barked more to himself than her. How had he fucked that up so badly?

"Maybe," Isa started, "you had something else to do at ten and got it confused with being here at the same time? It is a bit early for lunch seeing as I just finished eating an omelet."

He had thought the same but… Could he have gotten the time wrong? That wasn't like him. He'd never missed a meeting before or been overly early. Part of his reputation was based on his prompt business professionalism, including not wasting other's time. He'd have to figure out how he'd made this type of mistake and fix it.

Looking like an idiot in front of her had never been part of the plans. He shoved his hands in his pockets and wondered what to say. He wanted badly to spend more time with her, but he knew pushing her too fast would get him nowhere.

Taking things slow with Isaline was killing him. He knew she'd disliked him and was still wary of him. He needed her to give him a chance and get to know him better or keeping her was never going to work. There was no room for failure. She was his mate.

"Well, since you're here, would you like to go with me?" she asked, snuggling into her coat.

Yes. He'd go anywhere with her but decided looking desperate wasn't going to work in his favor. "Where?"

"I'm filling in for a skating coach down at the rink this morning."

"Skating? I didn't know you roller skated," he said, surprised.

She headed for a Jeep away from his rental. "No, silly. Ice skating."

Even more impressive. He'd tried to ice skate once in the rink the city built each winter at the Rockefeller Center. He took one step onto the ice and next he knew, he was staring up at the skyscrapers from his back.

In fact, that's where he spent most of that outing. After that, he decided ice skating wasn't for him. No matter how much Storm's kids tried to get him to do it.

She gave him a quick smile once they were in her Jeep. "I'd like to drive today."

Nestled in her old Jeep, seat belts strapped on, they pulled onto the quiet street. In the town, he'd been lucky and kept private parking at the entrance of his hotel. Otherwise, he'd never been able to pull out of a parking garage without waiting for the dense traffic to stop. Or worse yet, wait on someone's kindness to let him cut into the line.

Before he had a chance make small talk, Isa's phone rang. She apologized. "It's my sister. I really need to take this. Do you mind?"

He shook his head. "No, go ahead. Both my mother and sister would kill me if I didn't answer their call."

Isaline pressed the button on her steering wheel and an older voice came through the speakers. He wanted to give her as much privacy as he could, so he tuned out and studied the town around him as they drove.

Most of the houses were neat and tidy with small front yards. Many had covered porches with rocking chairs or bench swings and almost everyone had an American flag or Americana displayed in some fashion. How long had it been since he'd seen a flag outside of TV or a ballgame?

A couple of places he noted would be great

for a commercial building. He could imagine bringing in a big box store, or better yet, a mall to the area. They'd have to tear down several houses for the parking lot. Still, he'd give them a great price for their properties.

Maybe a hotel or a large movie establishment would be great. With his latest project, he had expansion already on his mind. Never too early to think ahead when it came to business growth.

And small towns like these were dying for new things and corporations to come in. There was not much here. She'd told him herself this was a small town with very little to see. He still didn't know how people could live such quiet lives in little places with nothing to do. The city was his place and he never saw himself in a town this tiny.

In the parking lot of an old building that resembled schools built in the 60s, a big group of kids with musical instruments marched in formation. He wondered if they were practicing for a football game or parade or maybe competition. The massive high school Storm's children went to had a band, but he was never into that kind of thing. He wondered if Isaline played an instrument.

ELEVEN

Isaline said goodbye to her sister and asked him, "Are you musically inclined?"

"No," he said. "You?"

Shrugging, she said, "I played piano when I was younger. Learned to read music but had too much other stuff going on as a kid to do much with it."

"Can you still play?" he asked, turning to her.

"If you consider *Mary Had a Little Lamb* and *Chopsticks* as playing, then yeah." She laughed, and the sound tingled in his ears. He could listen to her joy all day.

Ahead, he saw flames shoot into the air in front of the fire department. Several kids stood around the fire. "What's going on there?" he asked.

"That's the fire chief and his monthly demonstrations. He works with kids and families on fire safety and what to do in case of a fire. They get tours of the trucks and equipment afterwards. It's really cool."

"I bet it is. That would've been great when I was a kid." Still, he knew if those kids saw his dragon shooting flames, they'd probably talk about it for months.

"Yeah," Isa said, "I can't imagine what it was like growing up in the city."

He was sure it was much more exciting than living here, but he wasn't going to tell that to her. Then a female in a light blue button-down and dark blue coat stepped off the porch of a house. Behind her, she pulled an oversized wagon with boxes. "Is that—"

"A mail lady personally delivering mail?" she finished for him. "Yeah, it is. If you look closely, you can see the mail slots in doors or containers on the porch for mail. Don't see that in the city, huh?"

"No. Our packages wait with the concierge, delivered by guys dressed in all brown who drive brown vans," he replied.

"Oh," she said, her voice quiet and soft, "I remember going to New York and being so overwhelmed. I don't know that I could go back with that many people rushing to get from here to there. I almost had a panic attack." She shook her head. "Hang on. I have to get gas."

Isaline signaled and edged the car into a gas station with one island pump with four tanks. The store at the back of the lot reminded him of corner Stop N Shops.

"This is where you get gas?"

"It's great, isn't it?" She obviously hadn't read his expression correctly. The place was so small, he would've missed it driving by. He slid his seat belt off, going to offer to work the machine for her, but she jumped out of the driver's seat. "I got it. You sit tight where it's warm."

He couldn't get a word out before the driver's door closed. He looked around, noting the place could use a facelift but was clean and well lit. A lady coming out the store's door stopped to talk with a lady coming in. They hugged for a brief moment then chatted away.

At the side of the store, a teen was helping an older gentleman put bags of ice in a cooler in the back of his beat-up truck. How many bags of ice had someone helped him with in his lifetime? Zero.

The driver's door opened and a cold-looking

Isaline fell into her seat, shivering. "That coldness cuts right to the bone."

He had to stop himself from pulling her into his arms and rubbing her until she wasn't cold anymore. He hated that she'd gotten cold filling her tank. Where the hell were the people who were supposed to do it?

Pulling back onto the street, she asked, "Want to see the most recent exciting thing to hit the town?" Her eyes were all lit up with excitement. Must've been something great.

"Sure."

She turned her palm up and gestured out the front window. There were coming up on an intersection with mom and pop stores on all four corners. Scattered cars parked along the street sides. His eyes searched for something cool and new, not seeing anything remotely close to that. His silence must've clued her in to his obliviousness.

"You don't see it?" she asked, disbelief in her voice.

"What would 'it' be?"

"Hello. The flashing yellow light?" she said like she couldn't understand how he'd missed that. He burst out laughing. She smiled along with him, signaling her poking fun at him. "You know how long we've been waiting for this?" He couldn't imagine. "Years," she replied. "Now we feel like a real town."

He couldn't stop laughing at her playfulness. "Nah, really," she continued, "we're not sure why the county even bothered. Everyone here follows the stop sign. Haven't had any wrecks at this intersection in forever." Flipping the turn signal again, she said. "And here we are."

"Here" was a warehouse-like building next to a park that would've been a great place for a customer retail pavilion. He could see businesses lined up along the edge, offering all kinds of knickknacks, beverages, sweets, and other souvenir type items.

She gathered a couple bags from the back and climbed from the car. He followed her inside the ice rink front entrance where she was promptly attacked by a horde of squealing ten-year-old girls. He froze in his tracks.

The girls all spoke at once, vying for her attention while dragging her away. She glanced back at him with a "sorry about this" expression and he chuckled, waving her on. This was her thing, and he was just tagging along.

At a distance, he followed the gaggle of girls through a set of glass doors into the ice rink area. Women a bit older than he looked sat throughout the benches in the skate exchange area. The younger kids swarmed Isa while she laced up her skates. He made his way to an empty bench close to the front to watch.

He heard one of the girls beg, "Please, Miss Isa? I have the CD all set up." Then all the little ladies chimed in with *pleeeeease*.

Isaline glanced at him, her cheeks had a warm, rosy color. Was she blushing? What did the girls want her to do with a CD? He smiled an encouragement to her to do whatever the tweens wanted. Isaline turned back to the sprawl and told them yes. They erupted into cheers.

The group scattered, Isaline stood, and his eyeballs almost fell out of his head. She had taken off her long winter coat to reveal her outfit. His eyes skimmed from her white skates, up her pumped calves and curvaceous thighs to her skin-tight leotard with very short skirt. It was a short trip from there to imagine her naked and in his bed. Holy fuck, she looked good enough to eat.

Her full breasts stretched the top of her colorful suit. He wanted to peel the material away, replacing it with his mouth around her hardened nipple. His dick was quickly filling with blood. He groaned quietly, realizing he was surrounded by females who wouldn't miss a hard-on in his suit pants.

Fuck, if this was his reaction to seeing her wearing something sexy, he couldn't imagine how seeing her naked would turn out.

TWELVE

Beast straightened his tie to take his mind off the desirous image skating into the rink. The form-fitting skate outfit Isa wore drove him and his dragon bonkers. He moved around on the bench, trying to get comfortable with a raging hard-on. So not happening.

He couldn't take his eyes off her when she glided along, stretching her legs and body. Some of those stretches he wanted to try in bed with her. Shit, that was the wrong thing to think. She stopped in the middle and nodded toward the girls lined along the rink wall.

Music blared from overhead speakers, catching him off guard. Then what was happening hit him. She was going to perform a routine.

And then he recognized the music from the

Broadway musical named after the title of the song: *Beauty and the Beast.* How appropriate, he thought. She was a beauty. He couldn't deny that.

One of the young girls glanced at him with a shy smile then leaned over to whisper into her friend's ear.

With Isa's first push into a graceful backward glide, he was entranced. He realized for the first time when around her, his dragon was quiet, had stopped pushing at him to take her to their cave and claim her. It was as enchanted as he was. Speechless as the siren floating on air danced before them.

The music swelled to a high and Isaline launched into the air, spinning, then landed on one foot with the other straight out behind her in a backward gliding curve around the side. The girls clapped and screamed.

A couple of the kids glanced back at him and giggled. He felt a presence moving closer behind him and smelled soft perfume.

"She's so graceful out there," a soft voice said behind his shoulder. Without looking at the speaker, he nodded. She continued, "She's beautiful, isn't she?" He could only nod again—words were not in his brain for the vision. Isaline completed another jump, and the gaggle cheered.

"My daughter, the third from the left," the

mom rambled on, "has dreamed of being as good as Isaline for years. Isaline is her idol."

Wait, what? Someone idolized Isaline besides him? He glanced over his shoulder at the mom, only taking his eyes from Isaline for a second. "What do you mean?" he asked.

"Since you're accompanying her here, I'm assuming she's told you about her near Olympic career?"

"Are you kidding?" he replied. "She hasn't mentioned a word about that."

The woman laughed. "That's not surprising. Isaline's not the type of person to brag about herself or past accomplishments."

"Tell me more," he said, still watching the sight on the ice.

"Well, when she was a teen, she was good enough in individual ice dancing to make it to the Olympic trials. That's when my girl first became interested in skating. Isaline was magnificent in her routine. Nailed her jumps, stuck her landings, and should have been selected. Her family always showed such support. They were always here, always cheering her on and watching."

When the lady didn't go on, he had to ask. "Why wasn't she selected?"

The mom harrumphed. "No one knows, but my opinion is the judges wouldn't select her because she doesn't have the 'traditional' skater's body."

Beast couldn't believe his ears. Isaline was fucking perfect in body and soul. How could anyone want for more?

As if reading his mind, the mother said, "The judges wanted the women to be stick-like and look fragile. Deathly thin like runway models. Isa is healthy and has muscle, which is the image I want my daughter to appreciate."

"I can understand that."

The woman nodded. "For a while last year, Isa struggled with her weight, but she's been eating super healthy and has talked to the girls about the importance of nutrition and nourishing the body to be healthy and strong, not necessarily skinny. She's been so open about going to a nutritionist and doing different forms of exercise. Things to get the body moving and not get bored."

The mom laughed. "She's so funny. She admits she can't go to a gym and workout because she hates routines now so she does other things to get her workouts done. Being here is her favorite. She's such a great role model."

He fully agreed with that. He would appreciate Isaline's body all night long given the opportunity. The song came to an end and the angel on the cloud spun to a stop. The girls erupted onto the ice, racing toward Isa like a starving dog to a steak. They gathered around her, all whispering and glancing at him.

Thanks to his extraordinary hearing ability, he heard all their questions and comments.

Is he your boyfriend? He's really cute. How old is he? Have you kissed him yet? All things young girls think about when it came to boys. He found himself blushing, something he didn't do on a regular basis. What was wrong with him? He'd never been this timid around women before, much less a bunch of pre-teens.

Isaline smiled and glanced at him then shushed the girls. From there, they lined up to begin practicing. The next hour flew by as he watched her with the kids. She was a fabulous coach and the girls seemed to love her.

When the session was over, the girls skated off to put their street shoes on. The same mother who spoke to him earlier came up to him again. "Are you and Isaline going to some fancy event?"

THIRTEEN

"No," Beast answered. "Why do you ask?"

Her eyes skimmed down his body.

"No reason, really. You're dressed differently than most around here, so I was just curious. Have a great day." She waved at Isa and picked up the skates of one of the girls and headed out of the rink, daughter in tow.

Isaline came up to him. "Want to get something to eat?" she asked.

His dragon took control during his mental lapse from looking at the gorgeous woman in such revealing clothes standing next to him. He growled, "Yes." Knowing his eyes probably reflected his hungry animal's gaze, he looked away and cleared his throat. In his human voice, he said, "I'm always hungry."

When her brow lifted and her pale cheeks

turned pink, he knew she'd gotten his double-meaning.

"Give me a minute to change and I'll be right out." She grabbed her bags and hurried out the glass doors. With everyone leaving, he made his way to the lobby to wait. Within minutes, she returned in clothes that weren't as revealing as before. Which meant nothing since he had the image of her in that leotard imprinted behind his eyelids forever.

"Ready?" she asked, walking him to the door. He followed, still at a loss for all he'd learned about the woman in the past hour. He realized there was so much he didn't know about her, and he wanted to know everything. He wanted it all, down to the first time she said her first word as a baby.

In her Jeep for the second time, he waited till they were on the road before asking, "So, I hear you were an Olympian?"

She blushed and gave a soft, sexy laugh that made him mentally beg his dragon not to fight to take control. "That was a long time ago. And I didn't make the team, so it's not like it's a big deal."

"From what I heard," he started, "it's a huge deal to your entourage."

Her brows dipped. "Entourage?"

"Yeah," he said, "the pre-teen groupies drooling over you."

She laughed. "Those are a group of great girls with potential to go places with their skills."

"One of the moms said her daughter is skating only because she saw you and wanted to be just like you."

Her face flushed again. "Really? She said that?"

"Absolutely." He ran his fingers down her arm. "You're a rock star here."

"I don't know about that," she said quietly. He was amazed with her humbleness and how down to earth she was. So different from the women he'd dated in his past. So different than Rinelle LeFevre, the rich heiress that didn't even know where gas went in the limos she was driven in. Rinelle and others before her were so pretentious, so fake about who they were. Not Isaline.

"Tell me about you," he said.

She smiled and glanced at him, taking her gaze off the road for a second. "What do you want to know? I warn you—I'm really boring."

"I seriously doubt that." Just looking at her got him excited. She must've picked up on his energy and laughed.

"Okay," she replied, "I was born, grew up in a normal family in a small town, almost made the Olympic skate team, failed, graduated college, and got a job, occasionally bake and love feeding the homeless."

Beast couldn't help but roll his eyes. "I realize you were born, seeing that you're alive and driving." He almost added *and sexy as hell*, but now wasn't the time. "And small town is right."

Isa smiled. "Don't you love it?" *Love* wouldn't be the word he used, but— "This is the best town to live in. All the people care about others. They are willing to help without being asked and stand up for what they believe in. People in the city are snobbish and don't give a shit about anyone but themselves. Do you see people going out of their way to help others?"

He had to admit there were those who didn't.

"And how many times do city people flat out lie to your face?" she queried.

"Now," he interjected, "you can't lay that squarely on city people."

"Granted," she replied, "but you have to agree that those who work in the city will sometimes say whatever it takes to get what they want, truth or not. Especially when talking to strangers."

"Sometimes," he agreed.

"Okay," she said, "what about people who willingly give time or money to make other's lives better?" she asked.

He didn't think it was that city people didn't mean to *not* help. They just didn't know who needed help. "My mom is big into charity work. Every week, she goes to one of the soup kitchens to help out those who need it. She helps collect clothes for kids and families who need winter items and shoes."

"That's great," Isaline said and then gave him a quick, curious glance. "Do you go with her?"

Fucking hell. She would ask that. "No. I have a massive company to run, but I have a department that focuses on giving back to the community." And really, it seemed like he was always working. From when he woke, till he went to bed. That wasn't going to continue if this wonderful woman was to remain in his life. She laid a palm on his hand.

"It's not the same," she sighed, and he wanted to go out and do something to make her believe in him. Right then and there. "If you don't give your time and get to know those you help, you won't feel as good about the help you're giving."

"I see." He really tried to see things her way, but he was a busy man, and his company took almost all his time.

They stopped at a small Italian restaurant that had the best ravioli he'd had in years. Even going to the best restaurants in New York City, he realized this little town had gems that would make the town shine if only there was more to see.

"How's the business you came to town for going?" she asked as they headed back to her car after having lunch.

For a few hours, he'd almost had project Little Rose out of his mind completely. It was then he realized how dangerous Isaline was. She'd made him forget why he was in Full Moon Bay.

"It's slow at the moment. The client refuses to budge and I'm not changing my mind, so I might have to evict her."

"What?" she gasped.

He opened his mouth to calm her fears when a man walked up and interrupted their conversation.

"Isa?" The man hugged her and Beast growled.

Isaline pulled out of his arms quickly and took a step back. "Gavin?"

"Yes! It's me!" Gavin laughed. "I'm officially back. Did you get my flowers?"

Another growl vibrated in Beast's chest. His

dragon pulled at the controls, wanting loose. He'd burn the human to a crisp in a matter of seconds.

Isaline glanced at Beast with a worried frown. "Are you really back? I mean, I didn't really think—"

Gavin laughed and went to grab her again, but she pulled farther away from him. His smile dimmed, and he glanced from Isaline to Beast. "I told you I'd come back for you. I love you, Isa. Moving showed me that you were the only woman for me."

"I—" she glanced back and forth between Beast and Gavin. "Can we talk later? I'm busy right now, but we need to talk."

What did she need to talk to the human about? She should tell him there was no room for him in her life.

Gavin nodded slowly. "Ah, yeah, sure. I'm about to grab some groceries to fill my fridge. Want to come by for dinner later?"

She shook her head and glanced at Beast, then at Gavin. "I'll call you."

Something told him she wasn't going to say no to this man. The urge to tear the human limb from limb for daring to touch his mate almost made him shift on the spot, but he wasn't a hormonal teenager. Isaline was his.

FOURTEEN

Isaline growled as she slammed the kitchen door shut. He'd really returned. Why? What was the point of coming back when they'd never had a relationship that serious? At least not in her eyes.

"Someone's in a bad mood," her mother said cheerfully. "What's wrong?"

"Gavin really returned. I saw him just now."

Mirabel's brows rose. "Did a certain tall, sexy beast happen to be with you?"

She gave her mother an aggravated look. "Yes. I just don't understand where Gavin got the impression we had such a special relationship. For fuck's sakes, how could he say he loves me when we went on four dates and never had sex? Four dates."

Her mom nodded. "I understand, but maybe you should talk to him about it. I mean, he did come all the way back to be with you."

"Why?" She groaned. "I want to shove him back on a plane and send him back to Texas."

"Well, now, honey. That's not really how we solve problems."

She glared at her mom. "Really? And lying to people is? Don't think I don't know what you're doing."

"Whatever do you mean?" her mom asked innocently.

"Beast doesn't know you're the bakery owner. He met you and he still doesn't know he's met Mrs. Primrose."

"Bah," her mom waved dismissively. "A few days here will do him good. Besides, we're set to have dinner on Sunday. I'll let him know then that I'm not moving."

"Mom," she growled, "he's going to evict you. That is his building, you know. I mean he's offering you an amazing deal. Why won't you take it?"

Her mother gave her an unflinching stare. "I have a special contract and he's not getting my building until I feel the time is right."

"It's not your building, Mom. He's already

emptied out the rest of the lots. All he needs is for you to move and he can demolish and get to work on his new hotel."

"And turn this town into some sort of small version of New York City? I don't think so. His father never wanted that. His father wanted something special for Full Moon Bay and I'm going to make sure that happens."

Isaline's shoulders dropped. "You know what? I can't get you to see reason. I'm going to talk some reason into Gavin."

Her mom gave her an empathic nod. "Good idea. What are we doing for dinner?"

"I'll pick up a slice of pizza or something on my way home. Don't worry about me."

"I won't make tofu," her mom pouted. "I know you hate it."

She grinned and headed for her bedroom. "I know, but I really want pizza."

She was in her bedroom, readying to shower when her cell phone rang.

"Hi, Beast," she said breathlessly.

"Hi," he said in that deep rumbly voice that made her belly flip flop. "Got any dinner plans?"

"I was thinking of going for some pizza later."

"Sounds good. Want me to pick you up?"

She grinned at the fact he invited himself to join her. Christ. She really did like him if she wasn't bothered by the idea of spending the evening with him after being together most of the day. "No, I can meet you at the bakery later."

After she showered and dressed, she went to see Gavin. This wasn't going to be easy.

She knocked on his door and waited. A few moments later, he opened it and smiled at her.

"I'm so happy you came," he said, going for a hug again.

She stopped him before he put his arms around her and shook her head. "Can I come in?"

He nodded, his brow furrowed with confusion. "Yes, please. I'm glad my cousin stayed at my place. He's visiting his mother right now, so I'm able to move in quietly."

She stopped inside the apartment door and turned to face him. "Why are you back, Gavin?"

He stared at her, his eyes full of questions. "What do you mean? I told you. I missed you, Isa. I want you back and I knew coming home was the best thing for us."

She took a step away from him when he tried to grab her again. "See, that's the problem I'm having, Gavin. You and I were never in a serious relationship. We were casual friends. We went on four dates. Never got intimate and had two kisses. So where is all this coming from?"

He gave her a look of disbelief. "Are you kidding? We had so much fun and we were great together, Isa. We *are* great together. How can you say that?"

"Because it's the truth. I don't know what possessed you to come back, but I hope I wasn't the only reason."

His features turned stony. "What do you mean?"

She swallowed hard and side-stepped him, moving to closer the door. "I'm not getting back with you. I'm not. You and I had fun as friends. We tried to go further and it didn't work. It's over."

"But—"

She shook her head and turned the knob, opening the door and stepping out. "No, Gavin. It's over. It's been over. I've moved on."

"You can't move on," he told her. "I'm not ready to move on!" he yelled. Red splotches appeared on his cheeks and his eyes turned icy. "You and I are meant to be."

She gasped at his outburst. That was so unlike him. Gavin didn't get angry or scream. And he definitely didn't glare at her as if she were his enemy.

"No," she told him firmly. "We're not."

"Don't do this, Isa. We belong together." He gave her a renewed pleading look. "No woman in Texas compared to you. They're all lying whores, but you, you're the one for me."

"Would you listen to yourself? No, I'm not." She sighed and turned away from him. "Bye, Gavin. I hope you can find someone who truly makes you happy."

"You can't do this, Isa. I came back for you," he hollered as she walked toward the elevator. "Only for you."

"Move on, Gavin," she yelled over her shoulder.

FIFTEEN

She sat in her Jeep for a few minutes, thinking back on Gavin and watching Beast in the bakery. He sat at a table by one of the glass panels, working on his laptop. The suit was gone, replaced with a beige sweater and his hair looked wet from his recent shower.

For once, it wasn't perfectly combed. In fact, it looked like he'd finger combed it and had done a bad job at it. It was messy and so sexy. His casual look made her extra hot in the car. Not to mention the wet hair. Her girl parts warmed at the image of him in a shower. Lord have mercy.

He was so big and so sexy. And those hot glances he gave her only messed with her hormones. He'd been there a few days and the reaction he had on her body was as if she'd known him for years. As if he'd been hers for years.

She sensed a deep connection with him. Every hungry look he gave her fanned the flames in her blood. The desire that had been building even when she hadn't wanted it to grow deeper and stronger between them. It had been two days. Two. How could she feel this way in that amount of time? It was surreal.

How was that possible? This man was a stranger. No. Not a stranger. He'd been sharing himself with her and now all she had to do was find out more until she felt comfortable with him. If she could get him to see how important Full Moon Bay was to her and how badly she wanted to see it grow as a small town, not turn into a city, things could go further for them.

Do it. Give him a chance. Stop wondering what could be. Live for the now.

Fuck. She really was hearing her mother talk in her head. She needed to get her shit together. *And get laid. Get laid, Isaline. You need it.*

God. Therapy was her next step if her mother's voice didn't stop. She left her Jeep and chastised herself for her mental argument. Inside the bakery, she saw the empty chocolate-covered plate on Beast's table.

"Hey, I see you have a thing for the chocolate cake, huh?" Joy surged inside her. He liked her cake. It had never meant as much as it did at that moment that someone really enjoyed her baking. Oh, people told her daily about their love for her baked goods, but Beast was…he was different. She wanted him so much, it scared her.

Why did his opinion matter? Because she'd started caring. Maybe he'd leave after he got her mother out of the building, but for now, he was there. She wanted him to love her cake.

"I'm tempted to offer Mrs. Primrose's chocolate cake a spot on the room service menu of all my hotels. It's that delicious." He stood and slipped his laptop in its bag.

"Really?" she asked, her jaw hanging open. "You really think it's that good?"

"Good? I've had this cake for three days straight and it's not good, it's amazing. Decadent, but not overly sweet, silky smooth and moist. I can eat a whole cake," he told her without blinking. "A whole pan."

"You're being silly, but I think the baker will appreciate your words." She watched him pick up his bag. "Are you ready?"

"Yes. If you have pizza that rivals New York City, I may have to rethink my opinion on small towns."

She laughed and followed him outside. "You can drive. We're not going far."

He glanced down the street. "Oh, I didn't

realize that. I left my car parked down the street since I didn't find a spot here when I returned. You have so many rush times in this bakery."

"Yes. People here like their sweets. That's okay, though. I'll walk with you to the car."

He gave a sharp shake of his head. "No. It's too cold. You stay here and I'll get the car."

She almost debated with him, but he was being a gentleman again, and she liked it. Men didn't do things like that for her. Instead, she decided to embrace the moment. "Okay."

She watched him walk away and stood in front of the bakery, watching the snow fall in thick flakes. A few minutes later, he stopped in front of the bakery. She had taken two steps from the front door, when a loud thud sounded behind her.

Whirling around, she looked for what could've made that sound and saw the big broken brick on the ground where she'd been standing two seconds ago.

What the hell? A quick glance up showed her nothing. The snow was coming down and the top of the building was covered in snow. She couldn't see where the brick came from, but the building was old.

"Are you okay?" Beast asked, his gaze on the brick. "I saw it hit the ground right where you were. If you hadn't moved —"

She patted his arm and shook her head. "Don't even think about it. It's an old building. I'll have to get someone to check that out. It looks like one of the bricks lining the edge at the top." She stared at the place where the brick had landed. "Definitely don't need more of those coming down."

"Are you sure you don't want me to go look now?"

"No. It's snowing. It's best to wait for the snow to stop so a professional can look at it."

He glanced up again. "If you're sure."

"Yeah, now let's get some food," she said, tugging him toward the car.

"It's a shame you won't be driving."

She slipped through the door he held open and peeked up at him. "Oh? Why's that?"

"Yeah," he told her, his eyes a gold so bright, she almost had to look away. "I'd get more time to stare at your beautiful face."

A nervous laugh escaped her. "You're really good at that," she said. "Flirt."

"Why did you call me a flirt?" he asked once he got to the driver's side and sat, readying to start the car.

"Those unexpected compliments."

He shrugged and turned on the car. "It's the truth."

She bit her lip and gave him directions to the pizza place. This was the first time in her life she wasn't hungry after talking to a man for a while. Food had all but been forgotten now that he'd fired up other desires inside her.

"The restaurant is on this road. I'll tell you when to turn. I think you'll like this place. My mom's old high school friend married a man she met in Venice and he moved here and opened this pizza place."

He gave her a curious look. "Your little town gets more interesting by the second."

SIXTEEN

Isaline grinned. "It has its perks. We have good food. My biggest problem is having too many options on what to eat."

"I love your smile," he said suddenly.

The words were so unexpected she didn't know what to do. "My smile?"

He nodded, his gaze roaming her face. "Yes. It's full of light and life. I've heard of someone being sunshine. Now I know what that means. You're sunshine, Isa. My sunshine."

Keeping her gaze on the road, she managed to think while mentally picking his words apart. They were in a downtown historic district with old structures that had been remodeled to their original styles. Tall gables with square-tooth trim and fancy window displays lined the street.

"How do you like this area?" she asked, trying to bring back the easy conversation from before. "Instead of seeing the potential of what modern technology could bring, I want you to see past it. See the beauty of the past and duty to remember where roots run deep. This is what I love about this little town."

"I'm starting to see what you mean. What these places mean to the people around here— America was built upon the backs of blue collar labor workers who sacrificed for their families and those around them. Their goals in life had been to make the lives of those they loved happier and easier. This little town has it."

Her smile returned full bloom. "Yes. That's exactly right. Here, in Small Town America, that philosophy lives on."

He nodded. "I know. You're the biggest example. Helping others. Volunteering. Caring. Your need to help those around you makes you that much more interesting. That much more beautiful and selfless."

"Thanks. I hope you still feel that way after we eat. Turn in here." She pointed to the parking lot next to a hole-in-the-wall dive with a sign that read "pizza."

"I'm not even surprised." He laughed. "You don't do things based on looks, do you?"

She shook her head. "Nope. Some of the best things in life are found in unexpected places. You just have to be open to find the treasure that might be hidden under the rubble. This pizza? It will knock your socks off. Trust me."

"I do, Isaline. With everything in me, I trust you."

Opening the establishment door, she took a deep breath. "You won't regret it. Mmm."

"Damn, the marinara and garlic smell heavenly." He groaned. "I love pizza."

Staring at him with wide eyes, she led him farther into the restaurant. "Me, too."

When the hostess asked where they wanted to sit, they pointed to the same booth across the room. They looked and each other and smiled. "Stop reading my mind," she laughed.

"Good thing you can't read mine or you'd be running out of here a mile a second."

Yeah, she wanted to snort. If he only knew of the dirty thoughts she'd had from the first moment she'd set eyes on him, he wouldn't be saying that.

When the hostess set the menus down, Beast said, "How about an order of —"

"Breadsticks with extra red sauce," Isa finished.

He looked at her and gave a quick nod. "A woman after my heart, and stomach."

She simply smiled at him. Would they have other things in common? She couldn't wait to find out.

Resting an elbow on the tabletop, she dropped her chin onto her hand. "I love meatlovers—"

"With extra sauce and cheese," he answered. Her smile grew huge. "So beautiful. I'll never tire of that smile."

Butterflies made their home in her chest. She'd never felt so happy to be eating pizza at a hole-in-the-wall place. All her thoughts were now centered around showing Beast how amazing small-town life could be. Maybe he'd stay if he learned how much she truly loved it. Yeah, and maybe there really was a pot of gold at the end of a rainbow. She had to stop daydreaming and face reality.

"You seem preoccupied," he said to her.

"No," she lied. "I'm okay."

He smiled and his eyes flashed. "I can scent when you're lying."

She groaned. Fuck. That's right. Her sisters had told her about that. "Sorry. Tell me about your family."

"My mother is one of the sweetest women I've ever met. She loves to do a lot for others," he met her gaze. "Much like you do. It seems to make her happy."

"Do you see her often?"

"According to her not enough. She wants me to visit every week and to finally settle down and start a family."

Oh, boy. This was interesting territory. "And how do you feel about that?"

He sipped his soda and winked at her. "I'm working on it."

Dear god in heaven, the man was going to be the death of her. "I live with my mother," she told him. "I can't imagine not seeing her all the time."

"You've never considered moving away?"

She shrugged. "For the right reasons, I guess. My sisters moved when they married, but they found the loves of their lives. I wouldn't do it for less than that."

"Beauty and brains," he said. "Who knew I'd find that in Full Moon Bay."

She winked and picked up a breadstick and dipped it in sauce. "Stick around. You might be surprised at all you find here."

His hand covered hers on the table and the heat of his palm sent shivers down her spine. "I plan to. I've already found a gem worth more than all my millions. I'm not going anywhere."

"You say such perfect things," she told him softly. Unexpected and beautiful. Those words of his, she'd tried not to let them get to her, but she couldn't help liking the things he said.

Her cell phone rang at that moment and broke into their conversation.

"Sorry," she said. "It will be just a second." Then she picked up. "Hello?"

"Did you sleep with him yet?"

"Are you crazy?" she hissed at Zuri while not meeting his gaze for fear of what he might see.

"What are you waiting for? You want him. He wants you. You're not getting any younger. Live a little, Isa," Zuri told her.

"You sound like Mom."

"She's always been outspoken. Besides, Mom is right. You need to get laid. Get that sexy beast to tear your clothes off and show you what a shifter's made of."

Her face flamed with embarrassment. "Seriously. This is what you called for?"

Zuri laughed. "If you're nervous because he's so hot, liquor helps."

"I'm hanging up," she whispered.

"I love you. Not kidding though, trust your instincts. He is into you, sis. Give the man a chance. Get some tonight and crawl your way home!"

"Bye!" she mumbled and hung up, hoping she could act like that conversation never happened.

A quick look at him and she knew that was impossible. Then she remembered why. "Shifter hearing?"

His features were tight, as if he was having a hard time with his self-control. "And smell." He groaned. "God, Isaline. Your scent is driving me crazy."

Her desire grew listening to his words. He wanted her, and it was obvious he was fighting his attraction.

Live a little, Isa. The guy is tall, sexy, and you know you're dying to know what he's hiding under those clothes. Do yourself a favor and get him naked already.

She squeezed her eyes tightly and tried to stop the mental images of him naked. Too late. This was not good. She opened her eyes. His gaze was focused on her mouth. Nope. Not good at all. Then she realized what she was doing.

She was fighting a battle she was going to lose. He'd infiltrated her thoughts and fantasies.

Zuri was right. She needed to live a little. Or a lot by the way the vein on his cheek throbbed. Her underwear was wet, and she knew he could tell she was highly turned on.

"I want you, Isaline." He said the words in a low grumble that made her nipples hard.

"Let's get out of here," she mumbled, her gaze on his.

SEVENTEEN

The pizza was being placed in front of them when he asked for it to be boxed up along with their breadsticks. After that, they didn't speak. Tension curled around them like a rope, pulling them to move fast and get out.

There was silence in the car ride. She didn't bother asking where they were going. Not to the house she shared with her mother. That went unsaid. They drove to the next town over, Analai Hills.

"The Golden Dragon is one of your hotels?" she asked in awe as they readied to stop in front of the valet parking.

He met her gaze and nodded. Then he handed the keys to the valet and walked around to get her door. She tried to control her excitement and nerves but there was no use. Her palms were sweating, and her hands were shaking.

The Golden Dragon was a five-star luxury hotel that celebrities stayed at when they came to Analai Hills for the big Analai Indie Film Festival. It had gained popularity when big stars promoted it and now it was the hottest indie film festival around.

He grabbed her hand and led her into the hotel where everyone smiled at them as they headed for a private bank of elevators. He inserted a keycard in a slot that read Owner's Suite and the doors slid open.

The longest minute of her life was spent in that elevator. She had time to think about what was about to happen. Every time she wondered if she was moving too fast, he squeezed her hand in his.

The elevator opened to a large living area, but she didn't get a chance to look around much. She took her coat off and watched him from the corner of her eye remove his own, walk toward her and take it, tossing both on top of a beautiful white sofa.

Anticipation heated her blood.

"Do you want a drink?" he asked, his voice a barely-there growl.

She drifted to the giant glass wall facing the city below. This was the tallest building in Analai

Hills and all she saw was the snow falling and the thick clouds. "No, thank you."

In a heartbeat, his hands were on her shoulders, turning her to face him. "Tell me what you want, Isa. I'll give you everything."

She took a shallow breath and stared deeply into his eyes. "You."

Time stopped. His hands roamed down her shoulders to her waist. Then, much to her surprise, he picked her up, lifting her to near face level with him and pressed her against the glass, his body holding her in place.

"I'm all yours," his breath fanned her lips. She curled her arms around his neck, holding on and pressing her chest even closer to him. He leaned down, his lips taking hers and making her forget everything but how much she'd wanted his touch.

This kiss was…new. Different. Totally unlike the last quick touch of lips. This time, he took her lips and possessed them. Desire flourished inside her like a small flame being fanned with every swipe of his tongue. She gripped the back of his head, raking her nails into his hair and moaning at their mating tongues.

A soft growl reverberated from his body to hers. It heated her to the bone and turned her legs to jelly. Then he moved a few steps before sitting and she straddled him, her crotch right over his erection and her mind coming up with the fastest route to getting the rest of their clothes off.

Trailing kisses from her lips to her chin and down to her jaw, he sucked on her neck and nibbled on her shoulder. "Are you sure about this?"

She blinked at the haze of desire and leaned back, her gaze locking with his. Another chance to stop. He wasn't pushing. In fact, he was clearly having a hard time with self-control and yet he continued asking if she wanted this. Did she?

She barely knew him. Yes. Yes, she wanted him. They might not know each other like couples who'd been together for years, but right at that moment, it felt right. Her heart was full of warmth and desire for him.

Zuri had been right. She couldn't know if he was the right man for her without giving him a chance. At that moment, her mind and body were in full agreement of whatever may come.

Beast might not be her usual type, but he made her heart flip, left her breathless, and gave her more butterflies than any man ever had. She wanted to see where this could go, and she didn't want to stop.

"I'm sure." She brought her lips to his. "No, I'm positive."

She climbed from him and peeled off her clothes, pulled on the material holding her hair in a bun and stood naked before him, hair tumbling over her breasts. Normally shy, this was the moment she'd try to cover up, but she was frozen in place. His hot gaze roaming over her body ate her up.

"Now you," she whispered. "The sweater comes off."

"Whatever you want, love." There was hunger and pure possession in his eyes. It encouraged her to keep going.

The sweater gone, she got a chance to really look at him. He was corded in muscles. Strong and lean with a body that made her want to get on her knees and thank her mother for being a hard ass.

If it wasn't for that contract, he'd never have come to the bakery. Leaning over him, she tucked her hands into the waistband of his pants and pulled them down, freeing him. She hadn't seen a man this big before, but it didn't worry her. Beast was perfect.

There wasn't time to make a move before he was switching positions. She was now sprawled on the sofa with her legs wide open and he kneeled between her thighs, staring at her sex like she was a forbidden rule he was about to break.

He tugged her head down and kissed her. A kiss so intense and deep, it only served to make her feel mushy and romantic. He unlocked something in her. Something no other man had, and she wasn't sure it would go away, ever. He kissed his way down her body, to her belly and her hips.

God. His tongue was like a flame, leaving a wet, hot trail in its wake. She ran her fingers into his soft brown hair, gripping his strands for dear life as she felt his breath brush over her inner thigh. The first swipe of his tongue was enough to make her shudder.

"Ohhh."

"Fuck, Isa!"

She blinked and glanced down at his face between her legs. "What's wrong?"

EIGHTEEN

"Wrong?" his gaze never left her pussy. "Nothing. Things couldn't be more right."

Isaline let her breath out in a rush. "Oh."

"Your scent. Your taste," he groaned. "It's addictive. Like the sweetest honey being poured on my tongue. I can't get enough." With that, he shoved his entire face between her folds. Her pussy contracted, dripping wetness down to her ass. He flicked his tongue like a master over her folds. Up to her clit. Down to her asshole. It was absolute torture.

She moaned, thrusting her hips closer to his face.

Tension wound into a jagged ball inside her. He brushed his tongue over her clit in what she'd swear was motorized rotation. The quick flicks shoved her so close to the edge, it only took what felt like seconds before she unraveled. He sucked her clit hard and growled. The vibration did it. The ragged emotions twining inside her snapped like a rubber band.

"Oh…God. Oh, Beast!"

Pleasure consumed her, spreading like wildfire through her in a wave of release so powerful, she was left breathless. Her orgasm flowed over her in a rainbow of bright colors. He continued licking her, slowing his thrusts to drag out her orgasm.

"You're so slick and hot," he rumbled. "Watching you come has to be one of the highlights of my year. Hearing my name fall from your lips at your climax made me harder than ever." His deep voice shot pricks of lust down her spine. He stared between her legs. "Now I want to watch you come and call my name while I'm balls deep inside you. My dick will feel the heat of your pussy as I fill you with cock."

She licked her dry lips and sat up. "First, I get a taste."

His brows rose. She nodded and stood, switching seats with him and kneeling on the soft white carpet, she lowered her body between his open legs.

"Isaline," he grunted. "You don't have to,

baby."

She glanced up from his cock and watched a vein throb on the side of his jaw. "I want to."

He let a breath out in a rush. "Good, because I really want my dick in your mouth. I want to watch it slide in and out of your gorgeous lips. I want to see your blue eyes go dark with pleasure again."

She pushed his legs wider and curled a hand around his length. He was big. Hard. Silky smooth. And hot. She held his cock up to her lips and glanced at him.

His eyes were pools of fiery gold. "Suck me."

Her pussy creamed at his words. He slid his fingers into her hair, gripping a handful of the strands away from her face. She lowered, licking a circle around the head of his shaft.

"Ah, baby. We'll make this short or I won't last. I'm coming in your pussy. Your mouth might be heaven, but I know where home is."

She grinned and licked him again, this time sucking the head of his dick into her mouth. "That's it, sweetheart. Fucking hell, you're so good at this. Your hot mouth sucking me off is driving me insane."

Widening her lips, she took him into her mouth, using her saliva to allow him to glide down her throat. She did it slowly, having not done it too many times, she didn't want to mess up with him.

He grunted, squeezing his grip on her hair and shoved her face into his cock. "Yes, baby, yes. Just like that," he groaned.

Up and down she slid on his cock with her mouth. Her body felt tight with need. She glanced up, watching his abs tighten with each thrust into her mouth.

He moaned and grunted unintelligible things. She flicked her tongue over his dick, back and forth while hollowing her cheeks tighter. She swept her tongue into a zigzag motion under his cock as best as she could in the snug confines of her mouth.

He suddenly tensed and gripped her hair tight, pulling her off him. She met his gaze.

"Get up here. I need in you."

He helped her straddle him, holding his cock so she could slide down on him. Placing her hands flat on his chest, she pressed down, pushing him into her pussy. If there was a heaven, she'd just found it.

It was a slow slide down, but once her ass met his pelvis, she could barely move.

He cupped her breasts, tweaking and tugging on her nipples, adding a new bite of pain to her pleasure. "Ride me, Isa. I'm all yours."

She lifted slightly and dropped back down. Another lift and drop and the pleasure expanded inside her. She wiggled to get better traction and moaned at the different sensation from the shift in movement. Holy shit, she was never going to get off him again. Ever.

"That's right. Now move faster," he encouraged.

She rocked on him again, wiggling her hips in a wave, back and forth. She dug her nails into his chest, gasping. Her belly tightened. His tugging on her nipples made her pussy slicker.

"Lord, that feels good." She gasped.

He let go of her breasts, grabbing handfuls of her hips and helping her rock faster. And faster, until she couldn't do more than hang on and try to breathe.

She moaned, clawing at his chest from her coming loss of control. He gripped her hips harder, pulling her forward and pushing her back in a punishing rhythm.

"Beast…God…holy shit, that's…wow," she whimpered, hanging her head forward.

"I can't wait to see you come. To feel your wet heat suck my cock deep."

Slipping a hand down, she spread her pussy lips open, rubbing two fingers over her slick clit. She moaned and continued to rub, loving the instant heat that gathered in her channel.

"Fuck, that's sexy," he grunted. "Play with your pussy some more, baby," he ordered.

She did. After pressing her tiny nerve bundle hard, she lost her breath. Her world stopped. The tension inside her snapped fast, unraveling at light speed. Stars exploded behind her lids and a loud moan rushed out of her lips. A wave of pleasure shook her to the core. It sunk through every pore. Through every vein until it consumed her.

"Beast! God! Beast!"

He bit his fingers deep into her hips. She'd have bruises tomorrow, but who gave a fuck today? His hot, hard length continued to rub at her insides, scorching her ability to breathe. He grunted. Then he tensed under her, pressing her down hard so her pussy ground on his pelvis. His cock thickened inside her, pulsing as he came with a loud roar.

"Mine!"

The word was barely understandable, but at the same time he said it, fire took over her left ass cheek, making her squirm in place. He called her his.

A shudder raced down his body, so hard and strong, she felt it come through her, too. She fell flat on his chest, gasping for air and trying to get her legs to stop shaking. He caressed a hand over her hair and another down her back.

Afterward, he caressed the tender area on her behind he'd gripped hard enough to start a fire. "There's no turning back now, Isa."

"I wouldn't change tonight, Beast," she kissed his chin and sighed.

"I need to ask you something," he said softly. "Be my mate, Isa. There's no other woman who could ever take your place. From the moment I met you, my dragon and I knew you were the one for us."

"I need to think about this. We don't even know what a relationship would be like between us."

"Perfect. That's what it would be like. I'd give you everything." His hands slid up and down her back. "There's no other woman I want to eat like my last meal. Or watch come screaming my name. Or feel squeezing my cock with her pussy as I fill her with my seed." He groaned. "You're the only one I want that with. The only one I want to see have my offspring."

"God, Beast," she cleared her throat. "I…I need to think."

"I'll let you think, then. But I can't take back any mating marks. To my dragon, you're already his."

MILLY TAIDEN

She bit her lip and let out a sigh. "My mind is too hazy right now. Let's discuss this in a few days."

His fingers skated over her shoulder blades. "This is about forever. It starts now. You're my mate."

"I don't think—"

"Don't think. The world is filled with uncertainty, but I know you're the only woman for me. Your happiness is my new mission in life."

She shook her head, confused. "God, Beast. We haven't even discussed long-term yet."

"You can decide to turn me away, but it won't make a difference on anything."

She frowned at his glittering gaze. "What do you mean?"

He gave a soft growl. "You. Are. Mine."

Gliding higher up his body, she placed her chin on his chest. "Don't think that way. I don't want to turn you away. I have feelings for you, but I need time to figure them out."

"Take your time but know this: I'm not going anywhere. My mate belongs with me."

Did that mean he was willing to move to a small town to be with her? She should change the topic. He wasn't understanding her and she

121

didn't want to mess up the moment. "Your beard is growing."

"I'm sorry."

She raised her head off him and met his gaze. "Why? I like it. I like your hair not looking so perfectly in place, too. It makes you look more approachable."

"If you like it, I'll keep it."

"Thank you."

She slid up and kissed him, loving how hard he still felt inside her. Before she realized, they'd moved down to the soft white carpet and there wasn't time for her to think of anything other than Beast taking her all over again. Every way possible.

NINETEEN

Beast dialed Fierce and sat back to glance at the panoramic view of the city below. This was the first it hadn't been snowing. After the night he'd had with Isaline, he'd loved waking with her in his arms, but she'd quickly left to shower and dress, telling him she'd meet him at the bakery because she had a full day planned for them. He'd love it if the day was to remain in bed getting to know every inch of her body.

"Beast," Fierce chuckled. "I guess this call is to beg for my help, huh?"

"No. I have a job for you. Find out everything you know about Mrs. Primrose and my father. I want a copy of that contract they signed."

Fierce made a frustrated noise. "You know your mother has that contract and won't hand it over no matter how nicely I ask. She's said no multiple times. At the risk of pissing you off, I'm not asking again. She's likely to turn me into toast."

"Fine. Forget it. I'll give her a call."

"What's going on with the building? Have you made any headway with Mrs. Primrose?"

"No. I think she's playing games with me."

Fierce snorted. "She's been playing games with you. What tenant makes life this difficult? None that I know."

"Get back to work."

"Aye, aye, slave master. I'll let you know what I find out on this end about Mrs. Primrose."

"I have a feeling it will be interesting reading for me." He grinned.

After he ended his call with Fierce, he called his mother. He'd worn a pair of black jeans and a plaid shirt. He'd had to go to a local big and tall store to find them since none of the things he'd brought were as casual as what Isaline had told him to wear. Jeans. The last time he'd worn jeans he'd been in college. A smile tugged at his lips. She'd gotten him to do things he normally would've balked at. Leaving his hair messy, growing his beard. Even wearing jeans. But Isaline was his mate. He'd do anything for her. Anything to make her happy.

Another call and he was on the phone with his mother.

"Son! So very lovely to hear from you."

"Hello, Mother."

There was a loud growl that had him raising his brows. "We've been through this, Beasty. Mom. Remember? M-O-M."

He sighed. "Mom. How are you?"

His mother squealed like she did whenever she got her way. "I'm good. I'm so happy to hear from you again. How's everything at Full Moon Bay?"

"Mom, I need a copy of the contract Dad made with Mrs. Primrose."

Silence.

"Mom?"

"Why?"

"Because I'm trying to get the building emptied so I can move on with Dad's Little Rose project. Mrs. Primrose isn't moving and unless I can find out more about their contract, I won't be able to get her out without getting our lawyers involved and the city marshal."

His mother gasped. "The what? Are you crazy! You are not allowed to kick Mrs. Primrose out of there! How could you even think it!"

He grinned, expecting that reaction. "Relax, Mom. I won't go to those lengths if you send me the contract."

Silence again.

"I'll have to find it. I'm not sure where it is. You know how I forget things."

"You've never forgotten anything in your life, Mother. Don't start now." He knew it. There was something in that contract his mother didn't want him to see and he didn't know what it was. Now he wanted to see it even more. "Send the contract or I'll get to talking to our lawyers."

"Fine," she snapped. "Give me a few days to find it. I'm very busy with the children's charity ball tomorrow. Really, Beasty. I don't have all day to chat, son. I have to go. Ciao!"

Who would've thought that his mother would hang up on him. Things got more and more interesting. What the hell did that contract say?

TWENTY

Isa paced in the bakery office, waiting for Beast to arrive. She was so stoked for this surprise "date." Last night had been amazing. No man had ever done or made her feel the things he did.

But today, his reaction would tell her who the real Beast was—how true his heart was. If he was the person she thought, hoped, he was. You could never be too sure about someone until you saw them respond unprepared. With their guard down, the real face, the innate personality, would come out.

She knew he'd pass with flying colors, so why was she so worried, so anxious that something wrong would happen? Because she had feelings, deep ones for Beast. And if he wasn't the type of man that could give of himself without expecting something in return, she had to break off their new and fragile relationship.

Her small duffle bag lay on the upholstered chair, ready to go. Normally she didn't carry her tools in one, but they would give away the secret if he saw them.

A knock sounded on the door, scaring the shit out of her. She'd been so engrossed in her own world, she didn't see him arrive in the service area camera. Hurrying to the door, she took a deep breath and calmed her heart. His damn dragon nose would probably scent her worry if she didn't chill.

With a huge smile plastered on her face, she threw open the door. He wore a pair of jeans. Dear god, that man could wear the hell out of denim, a plaid shirt and a parka. He almost looked like he was from the small town if he weren't so commanding even in jeans. He looked like he owned the city. "Hey, good looking. You're here rather early again."

His face paled. She laughed when she realized why. "No, you're here at the right time, this time."

"Oh, good," he said, "I can't imagine telling you how much you mess with my head when you're around. I couldn't think straight before last night, but now I'm forgetting everything. Everything but you."

He leaned down and gave her a long, deep kiss. He had no idea what he did to her mind—and body—when he was around. She could almost drag him into a bedroom right now and have her way with him.

Man, that sounded good. Getting Beast naked and touching all his warm, hard muscles. No, more important things to do this morning. Too bad.

When he pulled away, she sighed, hating the loss, but excited for the next kiss and imagining them in bed again. "Ready?" she asked.

With a raised brow, he stepped back. "I am if you are." She grabbed the gym bag, the bottom hanging low with the weight. "What do you have in there? Rocks?" he asked with a grin.

She pulled the duffle to her chest. "Oh, no. No smelling or peeking. It's a surprise, sexy dragon." She winked at him, hoping this was driving him crazy for all the times he'd made her senseless. Had it really been only three days since they'd started talking and four since he walked into the bakery? It sure felt like a lot more time had passed between them.

"Oh, come on," he whined, "give me at least a hint. I can't stand not knowing." Desire flashed in the depths of his eyes and his lips curved into a wicked grin. "I'm good at bribing."

She laughed. "I figured so." Then an idea came to mind. "I might hold you to the bribe, but I will give you one hint," she said. "You're going to show me how good you are with your hands."

It appeared he liked that idea if his wide eyes and gaping mouth were an indication. He grabbed her elbow and turned her. "We're going the wrong way for that, babe. Bedroom is inside." She laughed again and swung him around to make a full circle.

"No, not the bakery. I've already had a taste of that." Her face flushed hot with that admission. At the car, he pressed her back to the door, his front against hers.

"How about more than a taste," he teased, his hand curved around her neck. The warmth of his palm and the hot look he gave her made her giddy with need. "There's a lot more where that came from."

She smiled. "And *came* we did. A lot." A soft growl emanated from him, vibrating his chest against hers. She tilted her hips forward against his hardening length, hoping the vibration extended all the way down. Where had this boldness of hers come from?

Good grief, what was wrong with her? They would never get out of there if she kept it up with her wanton ways. Was sex all she had on the brain? Hmmm. Yes. This had been mind-blowing sex. She didn't even need to think about it to know she'd never had sex that amazing. So, yes, she wanted more of it. Who could blame her?

Putting a hand on his chest, she pushed him back with what she hoped was a seductive smile. That's one thing she'd never tried to be. Sexy. Isaline was just herself. Always. She didn't try to seduce any man. But right now with Beast, she wanted him to lust after her like she did him.

Isa opened the car's back door and tossed her bag onto the floor. "Get in on your side," she sighed, "before I unlock the one door between us and inside."

His growl grew louder, and she laughed.

With both of them buckled in, Isa pulled out of the parking spot, onto the quiet side street. "Not many people at this time of morning," he said.

She scoffed. "You make it sound like it's before sunrise. It's nine o'clock." Shaking her head, she looked both ways before turning onto Main. She puttered along, taking in the details she never wanted to take for granted. King's Hardware came into sight.

"Let's stop in at the hardware store for a minute," she said.

She got another raised brow aimed at her. "Sure," he said. "Why not? All girls like to go hardware shopping before sunrise."

Isa had a hard time holding back her giddiness at his confusion.

After parallel parking in front of the store, she crossed the sidewalk as Beast held the store door open. With the bell tingling overhead, the older man at the cash register looked over. "Hey, Isaline," the owner said. "Good to see you this morning."

"Good to see you, too, Mr. King."

"You need any help?" Mr. King asked.

"Nope, we've got it. Thanks," she replied.

Beast leaned down to her ear. "You know where everything is in *this* store?"

She feigned shock at his comment. "Did I hear a touch of sexism there?"

He stepped back, hands up. "Not from me, you didn't. No idea what you're talking about. I didn't say nothing. I'm all for feminism and burning bras and hell, if you'd rather never wear one, I'm all for it. Panties, too."

Isa shook her head, grabbed a tie-around tool belt bag from the shelf and slapped it against his chest. "Here, put this on, Mr. No Sex Is Me." His gaping mouth showed up again. "Relax," she said as she turned and headed down the aisle, "Sex is me—sex-is-m." At his frown, she rolled his eyes.

"It was a joke. Would you rather be Mr. Feminism?"

"Hey," he said, "any sentence with 'no' and 'sex' in it is not a good sentence." Without a reply, Isa took a hammer from the selection and stuck it in the hoop on the side of the tool bag Beast had tied around his waist. She didn't feel like dignifying his comment with an answer. Even though she agreed with him. Boy, did she agree with him.

"What's this?" he said, looking down at the newest addition to his wardrobe.

TWENTY-ONE

"It's a hammer," Isaline said, adding, "You do know what a hammer is, don't you, city boy?"

"No, shit. I'm not completely city," he said with cheeky grin. "I've lived long enough that I get around."

"Humph," she mumbled, "we'll see." She turned down another row, grabbing a tape measure, Phillips and flat head screwdrivers—and laughing—snatched up a first aid kit.

"I saw that," he commented, eyes narrowing. "Apparently, you don't think I can hang pictures."

She laughed her way down the aisle. "Maybe.

It may involve hanging."

"Oh yeah," he scooted behind her, "that's what I'm talking about."

She reached back and slapped his chest. "Oh God, please save me from flirty dragons."

"You know you love it," he came back, his lips brushing the side of her neck. "Maybe I can convince you to wear this tool belt later and nothing else."

Glancing over her shoulder, she met his heated gaze. "Really? That's sexy to you?"

He stared at her lips. "I told you, I'm all for feminism."

"As long as it gets you laid, huh?" She rolled her eyes and continued walking.

"With you, whatever it takes."

She elbowed him in the stomach then laid her handful of tools on the counter. "Good morning, Mr. King."

"Mornin', Isaline," the owner said, ringing up the merchandise, "the usual?"

"Yep, a veteran today," she said.

"That's fantastic," he said. "We need a lot of those."

"Agreed." Isa snuck a peek at Beast to see if he'd figured it out. By the pursed lips and one narrowed eye, she took that to mean he hadn't. When Mr. King set the items on the counter, she stuffed them into Beast's pouch, screwdrivers in the middle. He said nothing, just watched her. God, how she wanted to burst out laughing.

"Thanks, Mr. King." Isa waved, and she dragged Beast toward the exit.

"Any time, young lady." Mr. King gave Beast the once over. The upward tilt of the side of his wrinkled mouth was enough approval for her. Great. He was winning people over left and right.

So far, her entire family was ready to hand her over to him without asking for her consent. Even Sage had called after Zuri and Mom told her about him. She was all for Isaline getting a shifter of her own.

After shoving him into the car twice—the first time, one of the screwdrivers in the tool pouch poked him in the balls when he went to sit. You'd have thought he was being murdered by the way he yelled—she hurried to her side and got the car on the road.

She glanced at him. "Any ideas yet?"

He made a big show of rubbing his chin and thinking. She could've punched him in his big, strong arm. Or glided her hand across his wide chest, down his flat abs to his— No. No. No.

Why was she torturing herself by hanging

out with him again? Oh, yeah. She really liked the big, sexy beast. With a sigh, she turned onto a residential street lined with vehicles. She parked at the back of the line. "Ready?" she asked.

He leaned over to try to look down the sidewalk, but she knew he couldn't see anything since they were so far back. Shaking her head, she grabbed her bag from the back, unzipped it and pulled out her own well-used leather tool pouch.

"Hey," Beast said, "why do you have a nice leather pouch and I got a dinky material one?" He stared back and forth between them. "I don't think that's fair."

She smiled at his pretend whining. "Because newbies have to earn their way to one."

"Newbie?" He snorted. "There isn't much in this world I haven't done in two hundred years."

"Really?" She grinned. "Awesome. I'll let you lead."

He gave a sharp, well-knowing nod. "Okay." Then his forehead creased with confusion. "What are we doing, exactly?"

Isa climbed out of the car. "Come on, let's get on site. We're late."

"You're supposed to wait for me to open your door." Beast hurried to catch up with her.

"I totally love that gentleman thing you do,

but we're in a rush now, Beast. Next time." Up the street, many people gathered outside a framed-out home. Men standing around a large box truck grabbed and carried items inside the house.

"Isaline," a lady called out. Isa waved and hurried her steps.

"That's Evelyn," she said to Beast. "She's in charge of this. In the real world, she'd be the main contractor."

"Contractor?" he repeated. They were finally close enough to read the logo on the side of the truck: Habitat for Humanity. "Of course." He shook his head and laughed. "We're building a house for a veteran."

"You got it, sweets." Isa hopped up on her toes and kissed his cheek. "Are you a newbie here?"

He smirked. "Unfortunately, I am. But that doesn't mean I don't know a lot of other things. I just usually pay others to build the hotels for me, not do it myself."

She snatched up his hand and rubbed her thumb over his smooth palm. "Yeah, I could tell you don't like to get your hands dirty."

He jerked his arm back. "Hey, I get my hands dirty," he sounded exasperated. "I just usually wash them pretty quickly." Isa laughed at how adorable he was. He grabbed her from the side, hugging her to him and poked her ribs. She squirmed and laughed. Chills ran through her from his touch. She couldn't wait for the time no clothes were between them.

They approached the woman who'd hollered her name seconds ago. "Hey, Evelyn." She gestured toward Beast. "This is—well, call him Beast." She could only imagine what Evie thought about his studly name.

She reached out her hand to him. "Hi, Beast. I'm Evelyn. Call me Evie."

He shook her hand. "Glad to meet you."

A bit flustered and pink-cheeked, Evie turned to her. "Isa, I thought you could work on hanging, taping, and floating since you're so good at that."

"Perfect," Isa replied. She loved working with drywall mud and the all the tools needed to make clean walls. It was a job that required patience and attention to details to get right. "Drywall on the truck still?"

"The guys carried in several sheets already. Plus a few boxes of nails. Whatever room they put them in is fine to start with. It all needs to be done," Evie said.

A crash sounded along the side of the house, turning them around. Isa saw several men on the roof and the ladder lying on the dirt. Two guys on the ground ran over to put it back against the outer wall. Yeah, working that far off the earth wasn't something she cared to do. All the shingle work, she gladly passed on to someone else.

"Sounds great," she said to Evie and grabbed Beast's hand, guiding him inside. "This will be fun. The only way to hurt yourself is smashing your fingers with the hammer."

Beast snorted. "Yeah, sounds great," he used her words with a hint of sarcasm. They walked past people doing various tasks from stuffing insulation between studs to sweeping up sawdust.

Stopping to look around to get a feel for the layout, Isa scanned the area. The concept looked to be very open with wider than normal doorways and no stairs. The veteran they were building for, or someone in that family, might have been confined to a wheelchair.

Pride and gratitude coursed through her knowing she could be helping someone who fought and sacrificed for the country. Whether or not she agreed with the politics of the war didn't matter. This person willingly walked into death's face so she, Isaline Primrose, could say anything she wanted, go anywhere she wanted, and live however she wanted.

Without these men and women who put themselves between American freedom and those who would gladly strip it away, the world

MILLY TAIDEN

would slowly be overtaken by greed, hate, and intolerance to the point that no one could save mankind from themselves.

Beast moved away from her, drawing her attention to a group of people laying flooring in one of the open areas. He asked one of the men a question and was directed to another guy in a red shirt. Isa recognized the red-shirted man as the construction head—the guy who had the blueprints and knew what was going on.

As Beast headed his way, she hurried to catch up with him. The grimace on Beast's face told her this conversation wasn't going to be a pleasant one. She wanted to ask Beast what the deal was but didn't reach him in time.

When she joined the two men, both were looking at the exposed rafters and roof. Beast said, "With that distance, you need at least one brace between those two walls."

The foreman shook his head. "According to the plans the engineers drew up, no support is needed."

"I'm telling you," Beast continued, "that span needs support. You get a heavy load of snow or any weight pressing down, and it will fall in no time."

"The roof is angled enough to keep most snow accumulation off. I'm saying it's safe," the

141

man said.

"You're not listening—" Beast's eyes began to show his dragon, and Isa put a hand on his arm to calm him.

"Hey," she said, "can we talk over there for a minute?" She pulled on him when he didn't move. Though she dragged him along, his and the foreman's eyes remained locked in heated debate. Isa guided him into another room out of eye sight from the rest of the group.

"Beast, if you're so worried about something happening, we can talk to Evie and have her take care of it."

Footsteps came into the room. "Have Evie deal with what?" Evie asked, making her way in.

Beast ran fingers through his hair. "I don't think the construction is as sounds as it should be."

"Why not?" Evie asked, her brows pinched.

"If you do the math," he said, "you'll see that the distance between some of the crossbeams is too much for possible stress loads. It will collapse with any substantial weight."

Evie asked, "You know this because..."

Beast hung his head. Isa wondered what he didn't want to say in front of Evie. Whatever it was probably had to do with his age or dragon. A reason popped into Isa's mind.

TWENTY-THREE

"Beast owns several hotels," she said, "all of which he's been involved with from the get go. Some built brand new while others he's renovated, and he sees this kind of stuff all the time." She flipped her hand in the air like it was no big deal.

Evie stared at her for a moment then nodded. "Okay, I'll talk to the construction guys and get them to recheck their numbers."

"Thank you, Evie," Isa said, hooking her arm around her friend's and walking her out of the room. "Beast just doesn't want anyone getting hurt."

"Sure. I'll call them now." Evelyn pulled her phone from her back pocket and walked toward the house's entrance.

Isa let out a deep breath and hurried back into

the room with Beast. "Is she going to call them now?" he asked.

"Yes, I think you worried her enough to take action."

"Good. I don't like what I see out there." He lifted a piece of drywall. "Let's start in here. I don't want you anywhere near that side of the house."

"Works for me," she said. Though she thought he was being a bit overdramatic about the roof collapsing, her heart warmed knowing he cared about the safety of someone he'd never met. "Set the board with the ends on the studs, then we'll hammer it into the wood."

From a container on the floor, she grabbed a handful of short nails and dumped them in a pocket on her pouch. When Beast place the board against the wood, she hammered in the first fastener and followed up with a second nail several inches above and below.

"So," she said, "how do you really know about the roof problem? Was my guess right?"

"Yes and no," he waffled. "I have seen a lot of renovation work, but that wouldn't have taught me what I know about stress dynamics and such."

"What did teach you about such?" she asked playfully, handing him nails.

"In the late 1800s, I worked—"

"Wait, what?" she cut in. "How—"

"Isa," he said, "remember, I'm two hundred years old."

She rolled her eyes. "Oh," was all she could think to say to that. "Go on."

"I worked with Wilbur and Orville Wright for a while—"

"Hold on," she interrupted again. "Wright as in inventors of the airplane Wright?"

"They really didn't invent the plane, but yes, the Wright brothers," he replied.

"What do you mean? All the history books say they did, at Kitty Hill," she said.

"Kitty Hawk," he corrected. "And they invented the three-axis control which enabled the craft to be maneuvered in the air. The wings and stuff had pretty much been worked out, though we did modify them to get them to work correctly."

She gave him a knowing wink. "I bet you have special knowledge about wings, eh?"

Beast stopped hammering and sidled up behind her, his growing cock positioned in the crack of her ass. "You bet I do. Why do you think I volunteered to help them?"

She wiggled her ass against him. He groaned and pushed her against the studs. She giggled at her teasing, then bent at the waist and pushed him back. If anyone caught them, they'd get kicked out of there for all that indecency. They needed to cool it.

"You volunteered?" That surprised her. She was used to people wanting to be paid for any work they'd done. That was one reason she liked this habitat organization—everyone gave without any expectation of repayment except the happy faces on the owners when they stepped inside for the first time.

"Well, I did have an ulterior motive, sorta," he replied. Nooooo! Her heart fell. So he wasn't the generous person she'd hoped. "I'd gotten tired of having to shift every time I wanted to go somewhere at any distance. I figured humans felt the same. Not the shifting part, of course, but the desire to travel and see new things and learn about different cultures. When I heard that a couple brothers were close to coming up with a design, I sought them out."

Maybe she was a bit hasty in her assumption. "What did you help with?"

"A lot of different things, really. The mathematical formulas they were using for lift were wrong as were the fine details needed for wing-warping. So I—"

"Wait. Wing warping?" she said.

"Yeah, that's the term I used so they could get it easier. When a dragon, or a bird, wants to change direction, we angle the tips of the wing to make our bodies roll left or right. I demonstrated by twisting a long inner-tube box they had at their bicycle shop."

"They had a bike shop?" Isa asked. "I didn't know that."

Beast snorted. "There's a lot of things most people don't know about the brothers."

"Like what?" She hammered in more nails as Beast thought about her question.

"Did you know that neither received a diploma for graduating high school?" he said.

She almost dropped her hammer. "No way. How could they be smart enough to figure out how to fly?"

"Life experience and a shit ton of trial and error." A sexy, sly smile slid across his face. "And of course, they had me, dragon extraordinaire."

"You're so not full of yourself at all," she giggled.

She lifted her hammer and pointed to the drywall. He continued nailing with his story. "Let's see. Orville was expelled from grade school once. He really didn't care for school. He dropped out before his senior year."

"What else?" she asked.

"Neither brother married, I don't think."

Isa gasped. "Were they gay?"

He chuckled at her expression. "You don't have to whisper it. It's no longer the 1800s and being gay is accepted for the most part," Beast told her with that humor in his eyes.

She nodded. "I know it is! I got caught up in the story."

"They were married to their work. I'd never been around two more dedicated people. They had a goal and they wouldn't rest until they had achieved it."

"Wow. I can't imagine being that obsessed with something." But she could see how easy it would be to become obsessed with one certain dragon. Hot, sexy dragon. "But how did working with planes and three-axis whatever teach you about math for stress on roofs?"

"With the boys, I learned the dynamics in the wind tunnel we built in their house." That got her attention again. "But the math part came later with Einstein."

Her brain stumbled again, and she stopped moving altogether. "You mean Albert Einstein? The smartest person that ever lived? $E=mc^2$ and all that?"

He picked up another piece of drywall and set it butted against the first one. "That would be him."

A squeal left her, and she wanted to shake the massive man. "Oh my god. What was he like?" she asked. How exciting of a life could one person have? For such a city person, he was turning out to be a lot more interesting than she could have ever imagined.

"He was certainly not like history portrayed him as," he answered.

TWENTY-FOUR

"No way." Isaline ignored her work, turning to him fully. She had to hear this. "What was he really like?"

Beast laughed. "He was quite the Romeo, sleeping around, even when married."

"Albert Einstein, the womanizer," she snorted. "Who would've thought? I didn't even know he was married."

"Twice, actually. His first wife was Mileva Marić. She was a fellow student of Einstein's. She was a math and science genius herself."

"Figures. Brainy people stick together," she replied.

"Hold on. They divorced," he said.

"That's a shame. Did they have any children?" Then she thought about what being the child of Albert Einstein would be like. "Were they all geniuses, too?"

His face turned sad, surprising her. "Their first child was a girl. I forgot her name, but she was born before they were married. It was kept a secret until about thirty years ago."

"How did they keep her secret? Locked up or something?"

"I think she died of some illness as a baby. Scarlet fever or typhoid. Something. Al never talked about it."

Isa snickered. "Al? What else about Al?"

"Well, even though he was a genius, he told me he didn't start speaking as a child until he was around three years old. Some kind of autism, I think."

Isa dropped her hammer. "Einstein had autism? What?"

Beast shrugged. "I'm not sure exactly what some doctor called the condition, but it wasn't unheard of at the time. And he could make a violin sing to break your heart. I'd never heard such music until he picked it up one day and started playing."

Amazing. She knew string instruments were some of the hardest to accomplish. It took years to master if one even did. "Go back to his wife. Why did they divorce?"

"What a mess his first marriage was. I don't know why they married in the first place. The had two boys—"

"Both smart as whips?" she asked.

"Unfortunately, the brains didn't carry down to the next generation. In fact, the second boy had been diagnosed with schizophrenia and stayed in an institution most of his adult life."

"How horrible." Isa's heart hurt for both father and son. "That must've been hard for the family."

"Al never talked about Eduard. I mailed several letters he wrote to his son, but I found out most of this from Millie—his wife's nickname. Eduard died in his fifties in a psychiatric hospital."

"I bet that put a lot of strain on the marriage."

Beast shrugged again. "I stayed out of that part of his life. But I know he offered her as a divorce settlement all the money he'd get when he won the Nobel Prize—and that was before he won it."

"What? How did he know he'd win it?"

Beast shook his head. "Don't know. Maybe he could see into the future, too."

"Did his second marriage work out?" she asked. "If so, maybe he could." By the grimace on his face, she could tell Al wasn't a psychic. "What's that face for?"

"Uh, well, his second wife was his mother's sister's daughter."

"Her what?" Quickly the family relations added up in her head and she understood his expression. "He married his first cousin? What the hell?"

Before he could reply, his phone rang in his back pocket. He pulled it out and glanced at the screen. "Hey, babe, I need to take this. I'll be right back." He walked out of the room, leaving her speechless. What else did her dragon man know? And *who* else did he know?

Maybe Beast would fit into her life. He didn't argue when asked to help with the drywall. He hadn't even smashed any fingers yet. He stayed out of Al's personal life, which told her he respected other's privacy and probably expected the same in return.

And then sharing his knowledge with two strangers wanting to make the world a better place for humans. Who would've figured the heart of this dragon would be as big as it was?

Could she see herself with Beast for the rest of her life? Abso-freaking-lutely! Especially if there was more of that intimacy they shared. That connection that seemed to be growing by the second between them. Was he the one? She really hoped so, because she was so close to going all in to the idea of long-term with Beast.

What would their children be like? That thought worried her. Would she give birth to dragons or two-legged babies? Either way, they'd be just like Beast. So perhaps that didn't matter. She'd think about that when the time came.

Then there was always his money situation. But he'd proven to be humble and generous. Not flaunting his wealth or flashing expensive things to impress others. If he ever did any of that, she'd dump him like a hot potato. She had no tolerance for braggarts or bullies.

Forever with Beast seemed so easy. He made her laugh, wasn't perfect, though he totally looked it, and the clincher—he loved meatlovers pizza with extra cheese and sauce.

Yeah. He'd asked her to be his mate, told her he could never see himself with anyone else, but she'd been sex drugged and hadn't answered. Now that she was clear minded, she could tell him she would be his. Only his.

His absence had been longer than she expected. She wondered if something was wrong. Sticking her hammer in the pouch's side loop, she went in search of him.

Throughout the house, more people had

come to work. With it being winter, most wanted to do inside tasks. Only the roofers were the ones in the cold. She didn't know how they all could stand being out there.

From around the corner, she heard Beast's voice. The anger in it stopped her in her tracks.

"Listen to me," she heard him say, "you stupid piece of shit. Do you not realize what you're doing? You need to fix this, or I will destroy your shitty excuse for a company." The words were loud barks, as if he were having a hard time holding himself under control. "This town doesn't need small businesses like yours—"

Isaline stepped back, shocked by his words and the heat in his voice. Who was he talking to?

She'd known he was a business man that could get his way and was no-nonsense, but the way he growled at whoever he was talking to was horrible. How could anyone bully another person that way?

"Isa?" Beast came around the corner and stopped. Anger flowing in her, she turned her pissed expression to him.

"Stay the hell away from me." She stepped back.

"What?" Beast's face was pale with confusion. "Isa...what did you hear?"

TWENTY-FIVE

Isaline glared at him. "I heard enough. I don't know what the hell was going on, but I can't believe you'd bully someone like that. Is that the true you?"

He stepped toward her. "No, Isa. Let me explain—"

She turned on her heel, headed through the home. "I don't want to hear another word. I don't care if you're amazing at what you do in the business world. In the real world, we speak to people with respect. That tone of voice and that anger, you need to work on yourself. Trying to intimidate a small business is not ever right in my book!" She stomped into the open area where several of the workers had turned at hearing her yelling. "I want you out of my town—"

Halfway across the room, a loud rent of

creaking and breaking wood come from overhead. The group working on the floor froze and looked directly up. Instantly, Isaline knew what was about to happen.

Terror driving her forward, she raced toward the group screaming for them to run, move, get out of the way. Then next thing Isa saw was daylight coming through the shattered deck boards attached to the top of the rafters.

The ground shook like a small earthquake hit them, knocking her off her feet. But she knew it was the impact of the top section of the house caving in. Right over the people working.

Screams erupted from the room in the habitat home, then sudden silence. Dust from the collapsed roof filled the air, hiding the devastation from those around the scene. Stunned, Isaline lay on the ground covered in shingles and pieces of wood. She didn't know which way was left or right in the thick air. Her lungs filled with debris and she coughed.

"Isa!" bellowed in her head. Someone was calling her name, but she barely heard it over the ringing in her skull. Sitting up, she continued to cough while scraps from the edges of torn material floated down.

Arms picked her up and carried her out into the fresh cold air. Beast set her down and brushed hair from her face while she breathed in clean oxygen. "You okay, Isaline?" He ran his hands down her arms, ribs, and legs. "Does anything hurt?" he asked. She could only shake her head, focusing on him.

He kissed her and leaned his forehead on hers. "God, you scared me, woman." He swallowed gulps of air with her. "Listen to me, okay?" He took her face in his hands and locked onto her eyes. God, he was so gorgeous even with white dust smeared on his face. "Here's what I need you to do. Get that first aid kit you bought this morning from the car. Bring it here so we can help until emergency service arrives." He tilted his head the side. "Looks like Evie is calling 911. First responders should be here shortly."

He helped her up. "Now go."

With panic barely held at bay, she ran down the sidewalk to her car at the end of the line. Fumbling with the keys in her pocket, she felt for the fob and pressed whatever button her thumb landed on. When she yanked on the door handle, her shaking hand slipped off, the door not budging.

Pressing all the buttons on the keyless entry, she heard the door locks pop up and grabbed the handle again. This time it opened, and she snatched up the kit and ran to the house. Sirens in the distance calmed her immediately. Help was almost here.

Coming upon the construction home, she gaped at the scene of almost half the house crumbled in on itself. People covered in powder either limped through the fallen walls or were helping others out.

She looked around for Beast but didn't see him. He must have gone inside to bring out the injured. Isa set her kit next to a man sitting on the ground, a gash on his head bleeding. "Anything hurt, Cam?" she asked, opening the plastic lid and pulling out a square packet containing an alcohol swab.

He shook his head, coughing.

"Good. Now, sit still and let me have a looksee at a little cut here." Cameron jerked a bit when she applied the swab to his wound, but otherwise he seemed fine.

"Your boyfriend there is a pretty stand-up guy," Cam wheezed. "I heard what the foreman said to him. I would've decked the guy right in the face."

Frowning, she asked, "What did the foreman say?"

"The bastard threated your guy to keep his mouth shut about something. Whatever it was, was going to cost the construction company thousands of dollars to fix and he wasn't doing it. Said the house was safe."

MILLY TAIDEN

She grunted at that. Fucking hell. Of all the times for her to jump to conclusions. Beast hadn't been threatening a small business, he'd been trying to make them be accountable and do the job right. Obviously, it was wrong. With all the men laying shingles at the same time—that weight itself was enough to bring it all down.

"Your man was mad at that prick and got right in his face. I don't know what he said, but it worked. The dick walked out, all red-faced and huffed."

She knew what her man said. He used whatever means he had to make sure the right thing would be done. And his capabilities included power and using his animal's authority to make it happen.

Scolding herself mentally for misinterpreting, she owed an apology to Beast the next time she saw him. This was another reason emotions sucked. They made her all insecure about how she felt and if she was seeing the real person in Beast.

A tall, wide-shouldered male stepped from the rubble with a woman in his arms. He carried the lady toward her and set her down. He quickly kissed Isa on the head, then wiped off the white powder covering his lips after the caring gesture. "Be right back, love."

Isa pulled out another pad, adoration and

161

pride churning through her for the brave man she'd chosen. She'd learned another thing about Beast. He went to bat for the little guy. Even if he wasn't interested in living in the small town, hopefully she could change that. He seemed happy to make sure those in it were living a safe life.

With each day that had passed, he showed her what an amazing man he was. And none of what was a part of him had anything to do with the money he had or the power he wielded. It was all him. Beast. The man she'd fallen for.

TWENTY-SIX

Standing outside the house while medical techs attended the injured from the roof collapsing, Beast glanced at the text from Fierce and laughed. He knew it.

He dialed Mrs. Primrose.

"Mr. Harte—Beast. So good to hear from you today. Have you decided to leave my bakery alone and move on to other business ventures?" she asked with hope.

A loud chuckle escaped him. "Not in this lifetime, Mrs. Primrose. Not in this lifetime. I need to change our plans, Mirabel."

"Oh," she said, a curious note to her voice. "Why is that? Isn't this contract important to you?"

He shook his head at the question and

glanced at the food tent where Isa waited for him. "It is. It's very important, but I have something else I need to do this weekend. How's Monday evening?"

"Well…I guess if there's no other choice. May I ask, what do you have to do, if it's not too nosy of me?"

"I'm taking my mate for a weekend date."

She gasped. "That sounds very nice, Beast. I hope you have a fantastic time."

He chuckled at how excited she sounded. "I will do my best to ensure she does. See you on Monday, Mirabel."

He sent Fierce a list of things to handle and then turned to the tent where everyone not injured was having lunch. She'd found an empty table where she waited for him.

"Hello, gorgeous," he said, kissing the top of her head. He'd never realized how much he'd missed out on not having a mate. Now that he'd found Isaline, he knew he couldn't live without her.

"Hey, I got you something to eat," she gave him one of those addicting smiles that lit up her face. "I need to talk to you."

He sat in front of her, watching as the tent started to empty out of those who ate before them. "What's up?"

She glanced at his plate and then at his face. "I hope a chicken sandwich is good? The food is donated by a local restaurant and we don't really get choices."

"Chicken is great. I'm not that much of an asshole to complain about food at an event like this."

She winced and bit her bottom lip. "Yeah, about that. I'm really sorry I said what I did before."

"Isa, you don't have to—"

"No," she stopped him, "I do. I've been struggling with my feelings for you and even though I know you wouldn't do anything bad, I let my insecurity get the best of me and believed the worst of you for that moment." She gave him a troubled look and the scent of her concern reached him. "I don't want you to think I'm judgmental. I'm not. What I did was wrong, and I should've asked you instead of assuming anything."

His heart thudded hard in his chest. From the moment he'd arrived, Isaline had never treated him like most people did. To her, he was like any other man. Not the rich and powerful Harte. To her, he was just Beast.

"Thank you for that, love. I understand." He picked up her hand from the table and brought it to his lips. "One of the things you'll never have to worry about, if you decide to give our relationship a chance, is us arguing, Isa."

She blinked. "Ever?"

"No. People can talk and resolve their problems without an argument. Besides, I care about you too much to ever want to see you upset."

A slow grin spread over her lips. "People have disagreements, Beast. I imagine we'll have lots of them."

"Probably. But your opinion should be valued as much as I value my own."

She leaned forward and pressed his hand to her cheek. "You say stuff that makes me feel all happy inside. Thank you."

"Don't thank me. I only speak the truth." His gaze locked with hers. "No matter what happens, Isa, know that your feelings are what's important to me. Some decisions are beyond our control."

"Today, I've learned so much about you and your past. I wish I had more interesting things to tell you about me. My desire to travel the world will happen one day."

He squeezed her hand. "Where's one place you'd love to go?"

"Egypt. The pyramids look like a magical

place and I love the history of them. I wish I could see all the wonders of the world."

"We'll make it happen, love. You'll see."

TWENTY-SEVEN

After a full day of helping build the house, they went to dinner. Then Beast drove her home and she couldn't wait to get a few moments alone with him. When she pushed her key into the door's lock, the door opened with just her touch. She stood frozen, knowing instantly something was wrong. Beast put his hand on her shoulder and pulled her back against him.

"I'm assuming you locked this before you left," he said.

"Yeah," she choked, "sure did."

He walked her backward then turned them around to the cars. He opened the driver's side door and gently pushed her in. "If I'm not out in ten minutes, you drive to the police station and bring them here." Beast headed inside.

Sitting there, coming out of her initial shock

and surprise, she started to feel silly from overreaction. This was her small hometown. Seldom did anything happened. *But sometimes they did*. Maybe she had forgotten to lock the door when she left. Maybe her mom had forgotten to lock it before she went to spend the day at Zuri's place.

Getting out of the car, she followed Beast's path inside her house. Why would anyone want to break into her mom's house? It wasn't like she had anything worth money. Her mom's most expensive thing was the car she and her sisters had bought her. Inside the house, things weren't old, but they weren't brand new, nor expensive.

There are still bad people out there, she could hear Zuri's voice in her head. She remembered the last time she'd spoken to Tyson Force, the town sheriff, he'd mentioned dealing with some break-ins, but she thought he'd caught the men who'd done it. Maybe he hadn't.

Before stepping in, she called out to Beast to let him know she was there. She didn't need him tackling her thinking she was an intruder sneaking around in the dark. When he didn't answer, she flipped the living room light on, and again froze in her tracks.

If she thought she was shocked before, that was nothing compared to now. Now she felt like she'd fallen into an absolute nightmare. This was her home, but yet, it wasn't. Complete devastation greeted her.

Her heart immediately squeezed in pain at the destruction. Pictures on the wall had been smashed where they hung, many having crashed to the floor. Table lamps were not only on the ground but crushed like someone took a Louisville slugger to them.

Furniture was tossed around, and seat cushions ripped with stuffing halfway pulled out. Her dad's easy chair, the one her mom had kept even though it was a thousand years old, but nobody had the heart to tell her to throw out, had been totally torn apart.

This wasn't a robbery. This was an act of vandalism. An act of hate. But that made no sense. Who would want to do this to her mother?

"Isaline," Beast growled behind her, startling her, "I put you in the car for a reason. Your safety."

"I know," she said, looking around, "but I don't understand." The emotional impact of seeing her living room trashed settled in. Unwanted tears swelled, and she wiped them away.

Beast wrapped his arms around her. "I'm sorry, Isa," he said. "Whoever did this is gone." She let him hold her. How would she tell her mother? A sudden thought occurred to her and she peeked at the kitchen door where her dad's old fishing rod still hung. It was in one piece. Thank god.

"Is...is the rest of the house like this?" She was afraid of the answer and squeezed her eyes closed.

"Let's focus on what's in front of us," he soothed.

Oh god, it was that bad. He walked her back outside to the car and settled her into the same place he did earlier. Then he pulled out his cell. He called 911 for her. Second time for emergency responders in such a short period of time. Hopefully, she'd never have to dial that number again.

She sat numb, her emotions settling, or she was going into shock. Beast knelt in front of her and took her hands in his. "Isa, I need you to think." She nodded, wondering what he wanted that made him look so serious. She liked him better when he smiled. His no-nonsense face was too sexy for any man to have. It melted panties instantly.

"Isa?" he said, bringing her from her thoughts.

"Hmm," she replied. She'd forgotten he was talking.

SAVAGE HUNGER

He sighed and scrunched his brows closer. His fingers brushed down the side of her face. "Stay with me, Isa. I need you to focus. The police will be here in a moment." Sirens in the distance punctuated his statement.

That snapped her out of the mental haze she had fallen into upon seeing the disaster of her house.

His smile momentarily brightened seeing her back to her old self, then retreated to his worried face. "Do you know anyone who would do something like this?" She shook her head. "How about anyone being mad at your mom?" Again, she shook her head. He sighed.

"It looks like some kids took batting practice at everything," she said. Kids could be so vicious. Especially when they were bored. The school wasn't too far away and there were a lot of kids who lived in the area. She knew for a fact her mother had no enemies. Everyone loved Mirabel. Maybe some angry teens decided to have some fun at her expense. That was the only logical reason.

The first police car turned onto her road, and Beast stood to greet them. She just leaned against the back of the seat and closed her eyes.

After an hour of answering questions and watching a myriad of people walk in and out of her home, she was asked to come inside by the police. Beast rested his hand in the small of her back, giving her his support through the ordeal.

"Isaline," Tyson, the town sheriff, said, "I'm so sorry about this."

She sighed. "Thanks, Tyson."

"Is your mother okay? I haven't seen her anywhere."

She gave a sharp nod. "She's been spending the day with Zuri and little Savannah."

His look was sad. "We've taken photos and brushed for prints. That's about all we can do for now. We need you to go through and inventory any missing items. Let us know what you find missing. It might provide clues to who did this." Isaline nodded. No words came to mind that needed to be said.

"If you hear anything or think of anyone that might have had reason to do this to your mom, let me know. And please, let me know if you need anything," Tyson finished.

"Thank you," Beast said for her and shook his hand.

Isa set her bag on the window ledge since that was the only place not damaged. Beast closed the front door after the police left. He took her into his arms again. "What do you feel like doing?" he asked.

TWENTY-EIGHT

"Like you said," Isaline replied, wanting to have the place cleaned up before her mom got home. "One room at a time." She made her way to the kitchen, the entire length cluttered with broken tokens of things she loved. From the pantry, she pulled out a box of trash bags. "You open a bag," she said, "and start throwing stuff in."

Looking around, she almost laughed. With such a mess, it would be hard to tell if something was missing or not. What a joke that would be. But she sucked it up and put on her big girl pants. Her mother would have a breakdown if she saw all her memories turned to garbage.

It was only material things. Stuff that could be bought again. This was what homeowner's insurance was for. Her mom had been wanting a new coffeemaker anyway. "Beast," she said, "I want one of those new coffee gadgets where you put a pod in and out comes an awesome flavored bean. No more measuring for me. It's time to get with the ages. Mom has been dying for one, and if now's not the time, I don't know when will be."

Beast smiled at her obvious change in attitude. "There's my Isa, full of positive thoughts. The incredible woman who amazes me every day with her strength." He kissed her long and deep. It didn't take away the pain, but it soothed her anxiety and filled her with warmth.

She batted him away. "No more of that until we have a path dug out to the bedroom. Then be ready, because tomorrow, we go shopping." What a great way to get over something that was so unfair. At least nobody was hurt. They were getting new furniture!

"What about when your mom comes home?"

She nibbled her bottom lip. "Let me call Mom and ask her to stay the night with Zuri. That way she doesn't have to be here for all this. I don't know how'd she'd take it."

"Good idea," he told her.

She watched him walk toward the living room and pulled out her cell phone from her pocket, dialing her sister.

"Hey, how was your habitat day," Zuri

greeted her.

"It was…interesting. Listen, I have bad news. The house was broken into and vandalized."

Zuri gasped. "What?"

"Yeah. It's a mess right now. Beast and I are going to clean up, but I think it's best for Mom to stay the night with you so she doesn't see this."

"Dad's fishing rod—"

"Still by the door. It's literally one of the handful of things that wasn't smashed to bits."

"Oh, thank god," Zuri sniffled. "I'll keep mom up here and break it to her."

"We'll get things into a better state so when she comes back, it's not full of broken mementos." She glanced around, realizing the amount of work she had ahead of her. "Just make sure she knows the rod is okay. Everything else is replaceable."

"Okay. Got it. Thanks for doing this, Isa."

She smiled, thinking of her spunky mother. "I love Mom. I'd hate for her to see this now. I'll talk to you tomorrow."

* * *

Isaline got home to find her mother smiling like she'd lost her mind. "Mom?"

"Oh, honey, did you see what Beast did?" She

did a full circle around the living room.

Once Beast had realized the job of cleaning up was too big for just the two of them, he'd gotten a professional crew in to clean things up. They piled photos that needed to be moved into new frames and emptied out the house. He then called someone else who met with her mother and Zuri and got information on what furniture she wanted so when she came back to the house, it wouldn't be empty.

He'd been on a mission. All day Friday, he'd been unavailable to her, making things happen. Now she realized why. Beast had gotten her mother's house refurnished. She gaped at the beauty of the furniture. The sofas had plaid pillows on them. The wooden coffee table was in the shape of a fish.

All the photos had been reframed in gorgeous new frames that had a lovely old look to them. The window treatments matched the tablecloth and sofa pillows. The entire house looked like something out of a country home magazine. The smile on her mother's face made her heart squeeze.

"You like everything?"

"Like?" Mirabel asked with wide eyes. "I love it! You have to see this!" She grabbed Isaline by the hand and dragged her into the kitchen.

There, where her dad's fishing rod always hung, was now a photo of all them with their parents on a fishing trip as kids. And the rod had been framed to line the area above the kitchen door.

"I don't know how he knew this was one of my favorite photos of all of us with your dad," she sniffled, hugging Isaline to her side. "I was scared to come home, but now I see there was no need. This looks so nice. Your dad would've loved it."

Isaline smiled and squeezed her mom's arm. "I'm glad you're happy, Mom. Where's Beast?"

Mirabel's eyes twinkled. "In your room."

Uh. Oh. Isa rushed to her bedroom, her mother following. She pushed the door open and almost lost her footing. Her bedroom hadn't changed much through the years. She'd never been one to hang posters or anything like that. Still, it had been outdated and not even looking the way she'd wanted lately, but this new room was unbelievable.

"Holy shit!"

Two people laughed, and she turned to see Sage and Zuri at the door, looking at her reaction with wide smiles. Her mom wiped at the tears on her cheeks.

Isaline loved traveling and had always

wished she could live in a beach bungalow. Somehow, Beast had gotten someone to turn her bedroom into a beach getaway.

The room had been painted a light blue gray that went perfectly with everything. From the seashells multi-panel canvas over her bed, to the sofa chair with sea star-shaped pillows in her little reading nook next to her bookshelf. A very cool nautical hanging lantern ceiling fan made her gasp.

To either side of her bed, she had very cool side tables with tiny seashells on the hardware. The bed itself left her speechless. It was a massive new bed. A four-poster bed. A bed she wished she could try out with her beast. The clean white sheets and pale blue pillows covered in tiny seashells and sea horses pulled a person in.

"This is amazing!"

"Beast, I told you she'd like it," her mother said, looking at Beast who stood in the corner, watching. She hadn't even seen him, but she'd known he was there with her. The curtains once again matched the bedding and she could only imagine it all matched her bathroom as well.

"This is freaking awesome," Sage said. "I get back and the house looks like it came out of an episode of Extreme Home Makeover."

She couldn't believe everything he'd done.

She rushed over and hugged him, pulling his head down to kiss him all over his face. Her sisters giggled in the background.

"Get a room!" Zuri yelled.

"We're technically in her room." Sage laughed.

"Oh, shush, you two. Don't you see they've missed each other? If you feel like you want to christen the new bed, we can leave for a while," her mother wagged her brows.

"Mom!" Zuri groaned.

"Ew," Sage said at the same time.

"No need," Beast told her.

Isa shook her head, not surprised at what her mother had said even one bit.

"What? A woman wants more grandchildren, you know?" Mirabel said.

"Mo-ther! You're going to make Beast run out of here if you keep it up," Zuri chastised.

"I have a surprise for you," Beast told her, his gaze on her face. "It would require us leaving for the weekend. How do you feel about that?"

"Beast, you've already done so much for us," Isa started. "I don't need anything else."

He cupped her cheek, rubbing his thumb over her jaw. "This is for us. Some more time to get to know each other. Or more ways for me to convince you to finally say yes to being my mate. You've shown me all about small town life. I'd like to show you a bit of city life."

"Go!"

"Do it!"

Her sisters said at the same time.

She rolled her eyes and glanced at the three women. "Seriously?"

"Young lady, you're getting your ass out of here with this lovely, tall dragon beast and if he wants to devour you while you're gone, then so be it," her mother said with a devious grin.

"Oh, god. Mom!" Sage made a face.

"I'll give you tonight to be with your family, but tomorrow morning, I'm coming for you. It will be fun. Trust me."

She chewed on her lip and frowned. "What do I even pack? I don't know where we're going."

"Just to New York for the weekend. I have something fun set up."

"You have to go," Sage told her matter-of-factly.

Zuri nodded quickly. "New York is one of the best places to go in the winter. It's so romantic."

"Yes," Mirabel said. "Go with Beast boy.

Come back and give me grandbabies."

Beast gave a hearty laugh. "I'm trying."

"Okay, let's go to New York for the weekend and be cold over there," Isaline sniggered.

"Smartass," Beast said, lowering his head and kissing her. This time, the kiss lingered, and she heard her mom and sister leave the room and close the door. If only they weren't in the house with them.

TWENTY-NINE

"C'mon, Sage, pick up." Isaline chewed her lip staring at the three outfits on the bed. Cell phone in hand, the facetime call buzzed in her palm as she paced.

With a melodic chime, the call connected, and her sister's face appeared on screen. "Isa? I thought you were in New York with Packed Pants Harte, making Mom's more grandbaby dreams come true."

"I am in New York. And don't call him that. Shouldn't you be making Mom's grandbaby dreams come true, too?"

"I already am." Sage snorted. "Honey, the man's first name is Beast. I think calling him Packed Pants is the lesser of the evils. Zuri and I actually tossed around calling him *Bulge Behind the Zipper Dude*, but it doesn't quite roll off the tongue the same way. Speaking of tongues, have you sampled his yet?"

"Jesus, Sage! You're awful. Forget I called…" Isa grumbled.

Sage grinned even wider. "Oh, c'mon. It's okay to dish it out when it's me? You called me, remember? What's up?"

"Beast sent up a personal shopper with racks of designer clothes for me to pick for tonight," Isa replied.

Her sister chuckled. "And that's a problem, how?"

"Sage! C'mon." She scowled at her sister's amused face. "I am so out of my element here, and you know it. You're the one with an amazing eye for fashion. That's not me." Isa exhaled, picking up a pair of fuck me pumps in her frustration and putting them down again. "He is waiting downstairs for me and I don't want look ridiculous. Not tonight. Not when we're in his neck of the woods."

"Isa, you've never looked ridiculous a day in your life, besides, he's seen you naked. Game over. You could wear a paper bag and he wouldn't care, not as long as he got to rip it off your body later."

Isaline exhaled. "I should have facetimed Zuri."

"Okay, okay…stop being such a big baby and show me the choices then," Sage shot back with a laugh.

Isa turned the camera phone around and smirked at her sister's long whistle. "Damn, that boy has good taste!"

"Sage!"

Her sister's laugh tinkled again. "Sorry… *uhm*…I think I'd go with the black knit dress and the knee high black suede boots. It's clingy yet classy, but still fun, plus it makes easy access for later."

"Leave it to you to make shopping X-rated. You've both turned into Mom," Isa smirked, turning the camera around so she could see her sister again. "If you must know, we're going to a museum opening or something like that, so easy access just hit a cock block."

Sage raised an eyebrow. "A museum? Wow. *Uhm*, fun? I guess."

"Sage, quit it."

Her sister chuckled. "Sorry, little sister. I'm just teasing, but remember it was you and Zuri who told me to live a little, so now I'm telling you. You're in the city that never sleeps, with a man who can keep you and IT up all night. You deserve this, Isa, so dress yourself up so he can undress you later. Live it and love it, babe. Don't think. Just do."

* * *

Isa fidgeted in the private elevator as it skimmed floor after floor on its way down from the penthouse suite. She checked her look in the polished chrome, smoothing her long hair as the car slowed to a stop. Sage was right.

The black dress clung in all the right places and fell to just below mid-thigh. Black tights and the black suede books made a seamless look that was sexy and sophisticated. No wonder she felt out of place. She gave her lips a quick press and then smiled, making sure there was no lipstick on her teeth before the doors slide open to the lobby.

With a quick inhale, she smiled as the doors opened, her eyes finding Beast's as he stood waiting for her. His hungry expression said it all, and if he hadn't looked at her exactly the way he did, she would have gotten back in the elevator and packed for home.

"Isa…my God, you're stunning," he murmured, taking her hand. He brought her fingers to his lips and kissed her knuckles before straightening. "The limo is outside, beautiful. Ready?"

She nodded, not trusting her own voice. Beast looked amazing. His tailored suit fit him perfectly, highlighting his broad shoulders and tapered waist. His dark hair was combed back, and the mischief in his eyes and the curve of his teasing smirk on his full mouth made her legs weak. His beard was shorter, but not completely gone which made her smile.

He steered her out the hotel entrance and toward the stretched limousine parked at the curb. "Metropolitan Museum of Art, Thomas."

The classy car sped up 5th Avenue in what seemed a dream. Beast's thigh was pressed against hers in the back of the limo, and all she could think about was lying back on the long plush bench seat and letting him crawl between her legs.

The car pulled in front of the MET and the driver came around to hold the rear passenger door open. Beast slid out first and then held his hand out for Isa. She got out and saw Beast standing like a metropolitan god in front of the museum's iconic steps.

"This is amazing," she murmured, looking up at him and then the billowing banners highlighting the latest exhibit. "Egyptian Kings...really?" she asked excitedly.

Beast nodded. "I remember you said Egypt was on your bucket list when we were at the habitat build, so I thought why not?"

She squealed like a teenage fangirl, and Beast

chuckled as he steered her up the steps. Isa held his arm and looked around. Except for the outside flood lights, the place seemed deserted. "*Uhm*, Beast, are you sure the exhibit is open tonight?"

He nodded again.

"Then either we're very, very early or very, very late, because it looks like there's no one here but us. An event like this should have crowds."

His lips pushed to a side smirk and his eyes glistened with obvious mischief. "You've never been to a Beast Harte exhibit. They're exclusive, and tonight's is as exclusive as it gets."

A valet held open the heavy front doors to the museum and the two walked in alone, their footsteps echoing in the expansive lobby. A runner made of sheer fabric patterned with a Middle Eastern design wound through the main entry area toward the back.

Beast swung his arm wide and grinned. "Ladies first."

Isa met his grin and stepped onto the runner as Beast slipped in beside her. "You're not going to tell me what this is all about, are you?" she said with a soft chuckle.

"Nope." He shook his head. "Tonight is all about setting the mood."

"The mood for what?" she asked, but before she could finish, the heel of her boot got caught in the runner and she cringed. She was going down. Hard.

Beast's arm shot out and caught her around the waist before she hit the ground. "Easy there, killer."

Embarrassed heat rushed up Isa's cheeks. "Great way to make an impression, Isa. Stumbling over yourself to your knees. Wow."

"If I wanted you on your knees, I think I could find a better way than booby-trapping the venue," he murmured, pulling her close. "In fact, I think I'd start by sweeping you off your feet."

He took her mouth, kissing her softly but with an underlying hunger, and then without warning scooped her into his arms.

"What are you doing?" she said, breathless as he carried her through the tall doors toward the main exhibit.

He picked up his pace, tightening his grip. "You'll see."

THIRTY

Isaline turned the corner and the room opened into something she'd never seen before. Priceless artifacts and statuary millennia old surrounded a plush harem-style tent, decorated with sumptuous pillows and silk veils. Fat beeswax candles gave the room a romantic glow, and Isa sucked in a disbelieving breath as Beast held her while she took it all in.

Large palms had been brought in along with stuffed lions and camels, their glass eyes hidden in the brush. The tent's interior had been set with low tables piled with fresh fruit and candied dates, nuts and wine.

"This place is unbelievable! Like something from a story book or *Aladdin*," Isa said, taking in everything.

He walked forward and laid her gently on a

tufted chaise, his eyes taking in every inch of her curves. He stepped back, letting his hand drift over her throat to her breast, lingering on the soft mound. There wasn't a soul around, yet her body hummed with need and fear.

"Beast, we shouldn't be here. What if we're caught? This has got to be a special exhibition tent and we're trespassing, not to mention ruining the set decorations."

He shrugged out of his suit jacket and tossed it over a chair, and then walked toward her again, unbuttoning his dress shirt. His eyes never left hers, and their normal chocolate hue had gone gold with his dragon. "You're right. This is for a special exhibition and we are the main attraction." He ripped the rest of his shirt from his shoulders and stood bare-chested, his wide muscled chest making her mouth water.

"Tonight is for us. For me. I want you wet and on display. For my eyes only. Spread wide for me to take and taste. There's something wild about taking you here. Like the queen you are. Mine. I want you here. I bought the space. There's no one else around, but it's easy to imagine us as an exhibit. A sex act on display."

Isa gasped as her nipples and clit throbbed from just his words. "How did you do this?"

His lips pushed into a smirk and he unbuttoned his fly and slipped his pants to just above his hips, showcasing that sexy V and a tease of black hair leading to the real beast just inches below. "I don't want to brag, but I'm kind of a big deal."

She reached for the front of his pants, hooking her fingers into his open waistband. "Big is an understatement."

"You have too many clothes on, Isa," he tsked. "What are we going to do about that?" He straddled the chaise and reached one hand out. With a low growl a single dragon's talon curved from his index finger and he hooked it into the neckline of her knit dress. One tug and the fabric ripped, the sharp edge of his nail slicing it from her body.

She moaned, arching back, her breasts exposed. Candlelight danced on her skin and he leaned down, taking one nipple between his teeth. He sucked the stiffening peak between his lips, letting one hand dip beneath the waistband of her tights. Nylon tore, the fabric popping and curling, leaving her pussy dripping and bare.

Stroking her wet slit, he slipped two fingers into her cleft and leaned in, taking her mouth. "I want you on your knees, Isa. Your ass in the air. You're mine. Every inch of you."

He broke their kiss and pulled back, taking his hand with him. Eyes locked on her, he licked her juice from his fingers. "Now," he said.

She scrambled to her knees on the chaise, and he tore the rest of her tights off, leaving nothing but her boots on. He pushed her knees wide and pressed the hard bar of his stiffening cock between her spanned legs.

"Now who's got too many clothes on," she said, catching his eye from over her shoulder.

With a chuckle, he kicked his shoes off. Then he pulled a small bottle out of his pocket and tossed it on the cushions and pushed his pants the rest of the way off, his cock springing free like a dragon unleased.

The sheer size of the man shocked her again and she licked her lips, swallowing instinctively in anticipation.

"In my dreams I've fucked you every way I can, and now in the middle of your fantasy, your bucket list, I'm going to make my dreams a reality."

His voice was as demanding as it was the first time they fucked. Only now the heat of his gaze nearly scored her flesh. He stared at her, his eyes taking in her full ass and hips, lingering at the way her juice glistened on her inner thighs, wet and bidding.

"Do you know how beautiful you are, Isa?" he said, fisting her long blonde hair as it spread past her shoulders.

She closed her eyes and let her head drop back as he slid his thumb between her ass, teasing her tight hole. "So full and delicious," he whispered, letting his fingers slide farther to tease her wet folds and circle her clit.

Beast reached around to her stiffening peaks, teasing circles over each as Isa arched back, moaning as his fingers worked between her pussy and her ass. He slid his hand down her belly, cupping her sex. "Spread this fine pussy wide so I can lick you from your wet, hard clit to your tight hole. Then I'm going to fuck you boneless."

She gasped, turning her face and he kissed her hard, his tongue demanding and ruthless. His palms splayed against her pussy, his fingers reaching deeper, working her spot as she ground against his hand for more.

Dragging his thumb upward again, he traced the fine seam of her ass until he reached her hole, this time soaking with her own juice. "You're so slick, baby. You're so wet, your pussy and your ass can take every inch of me, easy." He pulled her hips high, and she leaned her upper body down, leaving her with her behind up in the air. He spread her wide, dipping his head to her pussy and licked her folds, letting the end of his tongue curl as he plunged deep, sucking her wet juice. "Hot and sweet!"

Loud moans rushed past her lips. She whimpered. The feel of his lips surrounding her clit, licking and sucking her swollen flesh, turned into one of the most arousing experiences of her life. He flicked his tongue mercilessly over her bud and pumped his fingers in and out of her in short, fast thrusts. Her body was on fire. Her sole thought turned into rushing over that cliff that she knew would bring a world of pleasure.

Throwing her head back, she came hard, wetness pooling and dripping down his chin. A loud growl reverberated from his lips through her pussy.

"Mine, Isa. Only mine."

Isa's breath caught short and she came again, her hips bucking against his hand as pleasure crashed over her body. He pulled his hand from her drenched pussy and spread her knees wider.

"So sleek," he whispered against her ear, and he drove his cock through her slick entrance. Isa cried out, pumping her hips back to match him thrust for thrust. Her juices coated his cock and she took every hard bit until he was balls deep. Heat wrapped his cock like a tight glove, squeezing him.

He growled loudly, and the sound echoed against the empty museum's high ceiling. He slipped from her, but before she could protest, he fingered her tight hole. "You took all of me, your ass can, too."

Glancing over her shoulder, she saw him reach for the small bottle he'd tossed on the pillows before. Back on his knees behind her, she watched him grease his cock and jerk it at the same time. Her throat went dry. Watching him was better than any porn she'd ever seen.

"Like what you see?"

She nodded and licked her lips.

He dropped some of the liquid on her asshole and proceeded to rub it in and around her anal entrance.

"Ooooh," she moaned as the liquid warmed with his massaging fingers. She slid a hand between her legs and started rubbing her clit. She shuddered as she sped up, flicking her finger over her clit. The combination of her stroking her clit and his fingers thrusting in and out of her ass pushed her to the edge very fast.

Before long, her body was winding with the feel of more of his digits stretching her asshole.

"Relax for me, love. Let me feel your ass tighten around my fingers." He cursed. "Yes, just like that. Fuck, you're tight." He groaned as he lubed her up more. "You're ready for me."

His fingers were replaced by his cock. He took his time, pushing slowly. Her body responded to soften at the invasion of his cock pushing its way into her ass. The stinging wasn't too bad. She was so turned on, it didn't bother her much.

"Are you okay?" There was concern in his voice. "Do you need me to stop?"

"I'm good. I mean," she panted, "I'm great. Keep going." She pushed back and he slipped all the way into her in one tight thrust.

"Fuck!" He groaned. "Perfect."

He slowly pulled back and slammed into her.

She whimpered and increased the play on her clit. She squeezed around his cock.

"Isa…"

She rocked her hips. He slipped back and drove in. Harder. Faster. In quicker succession. Tremors took hold of her body. Her hand shook as her body went taut. His drives grew in speed.

He cursed, the sound a loud growl. "I want to stamp myself all over you. I want my cum deep inside you, claiming you as mine. Only mine."

At his raw words, she gripped the side of the chaise and lifted her ass even higher, urging him deeper and faster. He plunged his cock deep and growled a feral, wild sound. "You're so tight! But you'll be even tighter double-stuffed!"

She licked her lips and glanced over her shoulder at him. He reached for something wrapped in a silk scarf under the chaise. It was a dildo shaped like a dragon cock. Beast held it toward her mouth and she licked it slick before sliding it over her belly to her pussy. With a flick of his wrist he impaled her with the flesh-feeling molded rubber, driving his cock deeper into her ass.

Her walls shuddered against both thicknesses. She unraveled, shuddering and gasping for air. The climax went on, prolonged by his deep plunges. Slick anal muscles squeezed at his cock hard. Her legs trembled, and she went weightless. Boneless.

His body tensed, and his head engorged, straining deep in her ass. With a roar, he threw his head back, letting hot jets pump. Isa tilted her head, her body responding as the double feeling swept her into oblivion.

They were both breathless and panting as he pulled the toy and himself out of her. He was gone for a moment but she didn't have the energy to stand yet. Turning her head, she saw him pour water from a beautiful jug into a small bowl, wet a hand towel and return to her. Much to her shock, he proceeded to clean her and himself.

After wiping them both down, he picked her up and laid her on a bed of pillows. He'd barely put her down when she pulled him on top of her, curling her leg over his ass and her arms over his neck.

"Beast," she sighed, staring deep into his eyes. "I want more. I want you. In me."

THIRTY-ONE

Beast had to talk the dragon down. The scent of Isa's climax and her continued desire for him was making it hard for him to control himself. He saw the need in her eyes. The usual bright blue eyes were sapphire dark and mirrored his hunger for her.

She held his cock in her grasp, stroking him and jerking him slowly. Already hard, he placed the head of his cock at her slick entrance and stopped, making her wait.

Her face was flushed under the dimly lit tent. So beautiful.

"Beast…"

"Shh," he lowered his head and kissed her swollen lips. She tasted like sunshine and flowers. His mate was absolute perfection. "Let me savor this. Your body. It's made for me."

She spread her legs wider, giving him more access and a better cushion to thrust into.

"What are you waiting for?" she moaned.

"This," he said. In a single smooth glide, he thrust deep into her. Her eyes rolled back and her lips parted, a soft moan leaving her lips. Her nails dug into his shoulders, pulling him closer to her heated body.

How much better could this get? Isa was so much more than he'd ever expected from a mate. Soft. Sexy. Beautiful. Kind. Generous. And the feel of her sex hugging his cock tight was absolute heaven.

He propelled back and drove forward, increasing in speed with every slide into her slick folds. The faster he went, the more she begged him to go harder. He could barely contain himself.

Then she was screaming for him to go deeper and he gave her exactly what she asked for. She thanked him by scratching and scraping her nails on his shoulders and arms.

"This is amazing." Her voice was filled with shock and excitement.

"You're amazing, Isa. Your body and how your pussy strokes my cock with every glide. That's fucking perfect."

She arched her back and rocked her hips

under him, meeting each of his thrusts with her own sexy rhythm.

"Beast," she whimpered on a shallow breath. "I want this forever."

He thrust harder, her words pushing his dragon to the skin. "I can give you everything you want, love. Forever." He drove deep, faster, plunging every bit of himself into her and stroking her pussy with his growing cock. And she took it. Took all of him. Every. Hard. Inch.

Fuck, her body was driving him crazy. He griped her thigh, holding her ass and squeezed. Her pussy tightened around his dick and he groaned at the delectable feeling. Her channel was sleek, wet and sucking him off like she had him in her mouth.

Her body trembled under him, growing tense and then softening as she came. Her pussy clasped his cock, jerking him with every spasm of her orgasm. She gave a sharp cry, her nails digging into his arms.

There was no more holding back. The flushed face, hazy eyes and soft smile on her lips as she came back down from her orgasm pleased him. He wanted her to give him more of those satisfied grins. That look of absolute bliss on her face did him in.

"You're amazing," she sighed.

"Be my mate, Isa. Tell me you'll be mine. That you *are* mine," he growled, thrusting into her in punishing drives. "Say the words."

The beaming smile still in place, she nodded. "I never had a chance, Beast. I'm yours."

"Fuck, yes!" he snarled, going as deep into her as possible with every thrust. "I want everything, Isa. Let me fill you with my cum. Fill you with my seed."

She blinked pleasure-filled eyes at him. "I don't use birth control, Beast. I could get pregnant."

A loud groan sounded from him. "Sounds absolutely perfect. My mate carrying my child in her womb."

Her smile widened. "What are you waiting for then?"

The edges of his vision darkened, and his body went on full breeding frenzy. He pumped into her in quick, harsh thrusts, going as deep as possible until he stiffened. Her pussy embraced and sucked his cock. Tight. Hot. Hard. He came, his cock growing swollen in her slick channel.

A loud roar sounded from his chest. His palm sizzled against her ass cheek. Fire raced down his body. He shot his cum deeply inside her, filling her once again with his seed. She now carried his dragon's mark and was full of his seed. She'd always be his.

THIRTY-TWO

Beast knocked on the front door of Isaline's mother's house. He knew Isa wasn't home and had to speak to Mirabel.

"Beast," she grinned, pulling him immediately inside. "Come on in. Isa is at the bakery."

He met her gaze and nodded. "I know. I'm here to see you, Mrs. Primrose."

She widened her eyes and then sighed. "How did you know?"

He laughed. "When I met you at the shelter, I recognized your voice from our calls. I also research all my projects. I found it interesting that your contract with my father wasn't kept at the company, but at my mother's home. I also wondered what the secrecy was with the contract."

"Okay, so you figured me out, but what do you really know?" she asked with a knowing grin. "Better said, how much do you know?"

"Not enough." He followed her to the kitchen. "I need you to fill in the gaps for me. You clearly have some special clauses and I need to know what they are and why."

"Sit down. Let's have some tea."

He sat at the dining room table, watching the slim blonde woman move around the kitchen. She wore a flowy yellow dress and her hair up in a ponytail that made her look much younger than she was.

"I need information, Mirabel. No more holding back," he told her.

She brought the tea set to the table, filled a cup and offered it to him. "I just made tea."

"Mirabel…"

"I'll talk. Make your tea." She prepared her drink and met his gaze over the rim of her cup. "What do you want to know?"

"What is going on with the Little Rose and your bakery? What's the link and why won't you move?"

She sipped her tea and nodded. "Isaline says she's agreed to be your mate."

His frown turned to a grin when she

mentioned his mate. "She has. What does that have to do with anything?"

Mirabel smiled. "Everything. Will you be moving here or are you going to try and get her to go to the city?"

He'd given that a lot of thought and realized a small town wasn't so bad. It had given him Isaline and he wanted her to be happy. "I figured we can split up our time between the two."

Mirabel's smile widened. "Perfect. I'll talk now. You don't remember meeting me, do you?"

He frowned. "No. I have a great memory. I am sure I'd remember coming to this little place before."

She laughed. "No, no. It wasn't here. It was in New York. My husband and I went there for the weekend. We were only there to meet with your parents about a lease because they never came here and I really wanted that lot."

He shook his head. "I would remember meeting you."

She shrugged. "Let me tell the story and see if it clicks."

He doubted it. He had a great memory and he didn't recall meeting Mirabel in the past. "Go on."

"My husband and I were in New York City. I

couldn't leave my baby because she was a newborn, so we took all three of our girls with us but left the younger two at the daycare your parents had for their employees. We were in your father's office when you came in." She paused as if waiting to see if he had any memory of that.

He shrugged and sat back. "I walked into a lot of meetings with my parents and people."

She nodded. "True. But did they all have a baby?"

He stopped a moment, going through his memories and remembering a faint one of walking into a meeting where his mother was holding a baby girl and cooing at her while his dad and another man talked business.

"She was wrapped in a blanket covered in pink roses."

Mirabel gave a slow nod. "That's the one. You walked in and went straight to your mother…"

"She was holding the baby," he said, reliving the memory. "She was so happy. I had to see who made my mother smile that way."

"So you asked to see the baby."

"Mom handed her over and when she opened her big blue eyes, I felt something."

She leaned forward. "What did you feel?"

"A sense of…family. At the time, I thought it was a longing for having my own family. My own children."

"What did you really feel?"

He realized at that moment what he'd felt. A connection to the child. A deep protective instinct came over him and he brushed it off as the need to find his mate. "Isa…"

Mirabel sighed. "That was her. Your mom and dad recognized the instant protective instinct you displayed. You didn't know she was your mate. She was a baby. What you thought was a longing for your own family, was your dragon letting you know your mate existed."

"What does that have to do with your bakery and the Little Rose Hotel project?"

Mirabel's phone rang. She glanced at the screen and pressed a button.

"Hello, Serena," she said.

He glanced up to see his mother on Mirabel's facetime. "Mom?"

His mother gave him a wide smile. "I knew one day you'd say it without prodding, son!"

"Serena, Beast would like to know what the bakery has to do with the Little Rose Hotel project."

"Have you told him about the meeting?" his

mother asked Mirabel.

"I did."

"Okay, I'll tell him this part." She glanced at Beast. "When your father and I realized Isaline was your mate, we had to ensure you found your way to her once she was grown. You'd told us how you'd love to own a line of luxury hotels in the coming years and we knew that in time, you'd make it happen." She smiled. "Your father was so happy to come up with this idea. Mirabel wanted to open a bakery. We wanted you to eventually find your way to Isaline, so we allowed Mirabel to have the lot and your father waited until we knew Isaline was of age before he started telling you about his Little Rose project."

"Why Little Rose?" he asked, still putting it all together.

Mirabel and his mom laughed in unison. "You gave us that one, son," his mother said. "You said no matter how many roses on her blanket, the baby was still the most beautiful little rose."

Mirabel nodded. "So I got my bakery and it was agreed that once Isaline graduated college, you would handle the Little Rose project."

"We didn't see your father's death in the cards," his mother sighed. "It delayed everything. But I knew he wanted you to find your mate. He came up with the plan, so I just pushed you to make your father's final wish a reality."

Beast sat up, realizing he'd been played. "So whenever you said Dad wanted the Little Rose project to be done at that lot and Mirabel not budging with the negotiations, this was all a setup?"

Both women nodded.

"I told Fierce to make sure you went to handle getting Mirabel to move the bakery," his mom added.

"And I explained to him that I would not deal with anyone but you," Mirabel said, taking another sip of her tea.

"We knew it was all a matter of bringing you both together. You can't fight true love." His mother smiled. "And if we're telling you this story, it means you've gotten your mate."

"I should be angry for you not being honest with me from the beginning, Mom," he said. "But I got Isa, and I can't ever be angry when she's the woman I've been missing my entire life."

"Oh, Beasty," his mom sniffled. "I can't wait to see her now. I bet she's just as beautiful as she was when she was a baby. I knew one day she'd be my daughter."

Mirabel glanced at the cell phone. "Serena, we'll finally be family!"

"I can't wait, Mirabel."

Dear god. Both women getting together. He might just need to take Isaline to the other side of the world when that happened.

THIRTY-THREE

Isaline glanced at her cell phone. She'd missed a call from Tyson. He'd left a voicemail stating he'd come by the bakery to talk to her about the break-in. Goodness. She'd almost forgotten about it with all the things happening lately.

She cleaned off tables and groaned when she stood straight. Her back was killing her. She'd let Beast twist her in so many ways and she should've known she was not a damn pretzel. Now she was feeling it. Still, even with all the soreness, she couldn't help but sigh in happiness.

"Look at that grin," Becky laughed. "I know the grin of a woman who got laid."

"Oh, shush," Isa chastised.

"Shush my ass. We're alone here. The rush crowd is gone, and you know it's super slow at this time. So...got anything you wanna tell me?

When's the wedding?"

"You sound like Sage and Zuri."

Becky raised her brows. "So there's no wedding?"

She sniffed. "Maybe. I don't know yet."

She pulled a chair up to the counter and sat. "Go take your break, Becky. I'll sit here and watch things."

"Shouldn't you be on this side of the counter?"

She groaned. "Fine." She took her chair to the other side of the counter and sat.

"I'm taking these boxes to the back," Becky told her, grabbing a mountain of pink boxes from the bottom shelf at Isa's back. "We have a big order to fill and we ran out in the back. The new boxes come in a few days."

"You're leaving me with a big empty shelf," Isa complained.

"You'll live," Becky sassed her and headed to the back.

A few minutes later, her mother came in through the front door, a big smile on her face.

"Hi, Mom. You're here early. Didn't you say you'd come when it got busy later?"

"I did," her mom said. "But I drove over with

Beast and he needed me to show him some things."

"What things?" she asked, curiosity in her voice. "Spill it. You suck at keeping secrets."

Her mom started giggling as she got to the other side of the counter and hugged her. "If you only knew. I'll let Beast tell you the story."

"Fine. Why don't you go in the back and make us a sandwich? I'm starved," she complained. "I swear I've got to make new visits to my nutritionist because all I'm thinking of is food today."

Her mom had just gone through the door to the back when the sound of breaking glass made her head snap to see a car coming through the floor-length window, straight at her.

* * *

Beast saw the car going through the bakery glass panels as he came out of the flower shop across the street. His heart stopped, seeing the destruction the car caused. Isa! He ran, dropping the bouquet of baby pink roses and hating the sound of the tires crunching on wood and glass.

People rushed to the bakery before he even got a chance to get there.

"Isa!" he screamed when he rushed through the door, bypassing the crowds. He hoped she'd reply and tell him she was fine, but there was no answer.

The crowd grew larger, and one moment, there was a man in the car and the next time he looked there was nobody. He shoved pieces of wood out of his way, knowing that Isa would normally be behind the counter. A counter that was destroyed and lay in pieces under the wheels of the sedan.

A surge of anger and fear rushed through him. He could hear Mirabel screaming out Isa's name from inside the kitchen.

"Oh, god, oh, god," Mirabel cried. "My baby."

Beast called on his dragon's strength and shoved the car away from the counter area. "Isa!"

"Find my baby, Beast!" Mirabel screamed, trying to shove the kitchen door open but it was blocked by debris.

People moved pieces of wood and glass. He shoved the largest pieces out of his way until he saw a bloody hand. His stomach dropped. With even greater speed, he pushed off all the wood and found her lying in the bottom shelf, glass all over her shoulders and hands. She had bruises and cuts all over, but he knew she lived because he heard her breathing. It was shallow, but there.

He picked her up and ran into a group of paramedics.

"Bring her out here," one of them told him. "We can treat her best in our truck."

He carried her into the truck and watched them put an oxygen mask on her. Out of the corner of his eye, he saw someone running across the street and getting into an old pick-up truck. He knew his mate was going to be okay, but he had to find the asshole that did this.

Mirabel ran out of the bakery then. Tears streamed down her face and she had bloody fingers from trying to get past the glass blocking her way. "Is she okay?"

"She'll be fine. Stay here with her." He met Mirabel's gaze. "I'm going to find who did this."

She nodded and turned to his bloody mate. "I'll make sure she's okay."

He ran into the middle of the street and shifted, uncaring of the fact he tore his clothes apart or that anyone would see him. He let the shift take him quickly, allowing his dragon free.

Quickly in the sky, he searched for the pick-up he'd seen. Doing a big circle, it took him a while until he finally saw it, speeding toward the highway.

He dove down, scratching at the top of the hood with his talons. The man in the car started shooting. He shot a plume of flame at the pick-up, but the man only sped up.

Police cars joined the chase, yelling over a speaker for the pick-up to stop. The guy drove recklessly, weaving through cars and causing a couple people to swerve to keep from hitting each other.

Beast dove again, peeling the top of the pick-up like a can of tuna. He saw the guy then, shooting at him with hate-filled eyes.

"She was mine!" the man yelled. "We were supposed to get back together!"

Beast's anger passed the tipping point. He slammed down on the back of the pick-up, blowing out the tires and stopping it in its tracks. The guy hit his forehead on the wheel.

The police surrounded the pick-up. Tyson, the sheriff, approached Beast, giving him a grim look.

"Let us handle him," Tyson said.

The guy in the truck shot at Beast's dragon, proving he was wide awake and still had bullets in his gun. He hopped over the torn roof and shot again, missing Beast.

"Put the gun down, Gavin!" Tyson told him, pointing his gun at him. "Stop shooting the dragon or I won't be responsible for what happens to you."

Gavin shot at Beast one more time before Beast slapped him with a wing, sending him flying. He hit a tree and fell unconscious.

Officers handcuffed Gavin and dragged him into the back of a police car.

Beast shifted to his human body, still full of anger and debating if he should kill the man who hurt his mate.

"He's wanted for murder in Texas," Tyson said, handing him a blanket from the back of his car. "He won't go free any time soon."

"What happened?" he asked, watching as Gavin was driven away from the area.

"It seems he couldn't handle rejection," Tyson told him. "He had an affair with his manager and when he realized she wasn't going to leave her husband for him, he stabbed her to death."

Christ. *He tried to kill your mate. Your Isa.* A loud growl emanated from his chest.

"Try to calm down," Tyson said. "His cousin turned himself in. He told us he and Gavin were responsible for the break-in to the Primrose house. His mother got him to turn himself in."

"It had never been random or kids."

"No," Tyson pressed his lips into a thin line. "I'm sorry. I know every time you think about Isa being hurt, you want to tear him limb from limb. In fact, I'm surprised you didn't, but I appreciate it."

"I thought about it. I didn't want to be gone long from Isa. I just wanted to stop him," he growled. "I need to see my mate."

Tyson motioned toward his car. "Come on. I'll take you to the hospital."

THIRTY-FOUR

Someone was hammering at Isa's head. She woke up with a flinch. Blinking slowly, she winced at the continued drilling in her skull. God. What happened? She turned her face to the left in the dimly lit room and saw Beast sitting there, holding her hand. Behind him were several get well bouquets. One larger than the last. She couldn't believe so many flowers were for her.

"Hey," she croaked. "Water?"

"Let me," he said softly, bringing a cup to her lips and tilting it so she could take a few sips.

"What happened?" she asked, clearing her throat. "My head hurts."

He nodded. "You got a concussion when Gavin drove a car through the front of the bakery.

"Oh my god! I remember seeing the car

coming at me and trying to dive so I wouldn't get hit, but something hit me in the head." She raised a hand to touch her forehead but found it bandaged.

"He's wanted for killing his manager in Texas."

Isa gasped. "What?"

"They had an affair and when she broke things off to stay with her husband, he killed her," he said, still holding her hand.

She shook her head and winced. "We went on four dates, but if he hadn't told me he was moving, I would have told him I didn't want to see him anymore. He was very clingy and was too attached. Always showing up at the bakery or the skating rink. It started to feel like he was stalking me. His move was the best thing that happened."

"Don't worry about him," he said, meeting her gaze. "He'll never come near you again. I'll protect you with my life."

Her heart warmed at his words. "I know. I love you, too."

"God, I almost went crazy thinking the worst. Don't ever scare me like that," he chastised.

She laughed at his words and glanced behind him, her attention caught by the cute stuffed dragon and giant pink roses bouquet. "Those are all so beautiful. Who are they from?"

"Zuri and Savage, Sage and Feral, your mom, my mom, Ike and Christian, and me."

She frowned. "Ike and Christian? But how? They're homeless."

"About that," he started nonchalantly. "After I met Ike, I realized he could be very useful in one of my hotels. I had him meet with one of my HR managers. He already had great references and had worked customer service before. It was a case of losing everything from living paycheck to paycheck. I have him working at the Golden Dragon."

She gaped at him. "You gave him a job?" She squealed and raised her hand to slap his arm. "Don't say it like it's not a big deal. This is amazing!"

"With his new job came a sign on bonus and moving help. Since he'll be management, he'll have paid business housing for a year. Christian will have full paid tuition when he goes to college. It will give them a chance to save up and get their lives together."

She wiped at the tears racing down her cheeks. "You're wonderful."

He shook his head. "No, love. You are. You brought me in there and allowed me to see that they only needed a chance to put their lives in order again. I only helped make it happen."

She sniffled into the tissue he handed her. "You're everything. My superman. I love you, Beast. My chocolate cake loves you, too."

He met her gaze with golden fire in his eyes. "You're the chocolate cake baker?"

"Umhm."

"And when were you going to tell me?"

She grinned. "Why, have you been missing the cake?"

"Hell yeah! I'll do anything if you make it for me."

She raised her brows and giggled. "Anything?"

A wink. "Anything."

She closed her eyes and smiled. Then opened them to look at him. "It's insane. In a week you managed to make me fall for you." She raised the hand he held to his cheek, scratching at his short beard. The clean cut, perfect business man she'd seen that first day was gone.

This Beast had on a pair of jeans and a plaid shirt, with a beard and wild hair. He looked like he could be Feral's twin brother. And she loved it. Absolutely loved both sides of him. The clean, sexy, well-dressed business man and the big, brawny mountain man.

"I love you, my chocolate-cake-loving Beast."

He pulled her hand from his face and brought it to his lips. "I love you, my Isa. My sexy baker."

EPILOGUE

"So, what exactly do you want to show me?" Isa asked in the elevator in his cabin located in the mountains of upstate New York.

"Remember how you were asking me about what dragons hoard?"

She blinked wide eyes at him. "Yes…"

"You'll see." He pulled her into his arms and kissed her. "Are you okay? Do you need me to carry you?"

She rolled her eyes. "I'm pregnant, not sick. I can walk."

"Come," he winked at her, "you're going to like this."

They left the elevator and lights turned on as they walked. She gasped at what she saw. "Oh my god. Is that?"

"Yeah. My dad and I both like collecting cars. Old cars. He started the collection and I added to it," he told her, striding toward the weirdest looking car she'd ever seen.

"What is this?" she asked, shocked at seeing antiques in his private cabin.

"My dad and I financed a lot of the first inventors, so we got to keep our own models. This one was built in 1769. It's one of the first steam-powered automobiles capable of human transportation. It was built by Nicolas-Joseph Cugnot."

She couldn't believe he had a copy of the first car ever built. "That's unbelievable."

They continued walking to the next display.

"This one was invented in 1808, by François Isaac de Rivaz. That one was from 1870 by Siegfried Marcus. He built the first gasoline powered combustion engine. He did quite a few of them in this line and all have advances from steering, clutch and brakes."

She blinked at the amount of history in his underground parking. "Wow."

"This one here is the first gas powered Benz, built in 1885."

"Like Mercedes Benz?" She gaped at the car.

"Yeah. Then Ford came along and mass

produced their first one in 1903. And the rest, as they say, is history."

She leaned into his side and hugged him. "You guys really like cars."

"There's something else I want to show you," he told her, pulling her down a hallway, away from the car to a massive two-foot-thick door.

"What do you have in there, Fort Knox?" she joked.

"You'll see." He dialed a security code and the door opened. More lights turned on and she gasped at the number of jewelry displays with blue gems.

"You have a thing for blue?"

He cupped her jaw and smiled. "Your eyes. They're the most beautiful blue and I didn't realize why I was hoarding every blue gem I could get my hands on, for the past thirty years."

"Since you saw me as a baby?" she asked, having been told the story of how they first met.

He nodded. "I didn't know why I started collecting blue gems, but I did. It became an obsession. I realize now, I was looking for something as bright as your eyes."

She tugged on his sweater, pulling him down. "You're too tall. Come down here so I can kiss you." He lifted her, and she curled her arms around him neck, kissing him deep and sound. "You're so romantic."

"Do you think your mother and mine are driving Fierce crazy?"

She giggled and nodded. "Without a doubt. Thank you for putting the bakery in the lobby. And I know your mom will be great at designing the interior."

"My father and mother came up with Little Rose. She needs to be able to be part of it. That was their project."

He carried her back to the elevator and the rest of the way to the living room.

She blinked at the bottle of apple juice on ice and the picnic on the soft carpet in front of the fireplace where they could watch the snow fall from the cabin's big panoramic windows.

They sat in front of the fireplace. "I thought you'd want a snack," he told her.

She grinned and picked up a piece of fruit. "I do. I can't seem to stop eating."

"You've been very good about sticking to healthy eating."

She shrugged. "I want to be a good role model for our daughter."

He got on one knee, pulling a ring out of his pocket. "You'll be an amazing mother, Isa.

You've made me immensely happy as my mate. I just want to go full circle and make you my wife. Will you marry me?"

She nodded and wiped at the tears in her eyes. "Your daughter is making me emotional. These are happy tears! I love you!" She threw herself in his arms and sat on his lap, watching him slide the ring on her finger. It was a gorgeous sapphire in a platinum setting with white diamonds to either side.

"It's not as beautiful as your eyes, but it complements them," he said, kissing her deep and stirring her unending hunger for him.

"Have I told you how you say the sweetest things?" She kissed him back, hugging herself tight to his body. Her heart filled with happiness. She'd found her own shifter. Beast loved her. He showed her every single day with his actions.

"You have," he said, tugging on her big fluffy sweater, "but I'd rather you show me."

"Have I also told you that you're a pervert?"

He grinned, pushing back into the pillows by the fire. "Every single day, love."

THE END

ABOUT THE AUTHOR

New York Times and USA Today Bestselling Author

Hi! I'm Milly Taiden. I love to write sexy stories featuring fun, sassy heroines with curves and growly alpha males with fur. My books are a great way to satisfy your craving for paranormal romance with action, humor, suspense and happily ever afters.

I live in Florida with my hubby, our boys, and our fur children "Needy Speedy" and "Stormy." Yes, I am aware I'm bossy, and I am seriously addicted to iced caramel lattes.

I love to meet new readers, so come sign up for my newsletter and check out my Facebook page. We always have lots of fun stuff going on there.

SIGN UP FOR MILLY'S NEWSLETTER FOR LATEST NEWS!

http://eepurl.com/pt9q1

Find out more about Milly Taiden here:

Email: millytaiden@gmail.com
Website: http://www.millytaiden.com
Facebook:
http://www.facebook.com/millytaidenpage
Twitter: https://www.twitter.com/millytaiden

If you liked this story, you might also enjoy the following by Milly Taiden:

Sassy Mates / Sassy Ever After Series
Scent of a Mate *Book One*
A Mate's Bite *Book Two*
Unexpectedly Mated *Book Three*
A Sassy Wedding *Short 3.7*
The Mate Challenge *Book Four*
Sassy in Diapers *Short 4.3*
Fighting for Her Mate *Book Five*
A Fang in the Sass *Book 6*
Also, check out the **Sassy Ever After Kindle World on Amazon**

A.L.F.A Series
Elemental Mating *Book One*
Mating Needs *Book Two*
Dangerous Mating *Book Three (Coming Soon)*
Fearless Mating *Book Four (Coming Soon)*

Savage Shifters
Savage Bite *Book One*
Savage Kiss *Book Two*
Savage Hunger *Book Three (Coming soon)*

Drachen Mates
Bound in Flames *Book One*
Bound in Darkness *Book Two*
Bound in Eternity *Book Three*
Bound in Ashes *Book Four*

Miss Behaved *Book Three*
Miss Behaved *Book Three*
Miss Mated *Book Four (Coming Soon)*
Miss Conceived *Book Five (Coming Soon)*

FUR-ocious Lust - Bears
Fur-Bidden *Book One*
Fur-Gotten *Book Two*
Fur-Given Book *Three*

FUR-ocious Lust - Tigers
Stripe-Tease *Book Four*
Stripe-Search *Book Five*
Stripe-Club *Book Six*

Night and Day Ink
Bitten by Night *Book One*
Seduced by Days *Book Two*
Mated by Night *Book Three*
Taken by Night *Book Four*
Dragon Baby *Book Five*

Shifters Undercover
Bearly in Control *Book One*
Fur Fox's Sake *Book Two*

Black Meadow Pack
Sharp Change *Black Meadows Pack Book One*
Caged Heat *Black Meadows Pack Book Two*

Other Works
Wolf Fever
Fate's Wish
Wynter's Captive
Sinfully Naughty Vol. 1
Don't Drink and Hex
Hex Gone Wild
Hex and Kisses
Alpha Owned
Match Made in Hell
Alpha Geek

HOWLS Romances
The Wolf's Royal Baby
Her Fairytale Wolf *Co-Written*
The Wolf's Dream Mate *Co-Written*
Her Winter Wolves *Co-Written*

Contemporary Works
Lucky Chase
Their Second Chance
Club Duo Boxed Set
A Hero's Pride
A Hero Scarred
A Hero for Sale
Wounded Soldiers Set

If you enjoyed the book, please consider leaving a review, even if it's only a line or two; it would make all the difference and would be very much appreciated.

Thank you!

Made in the USA
Columbia, SC
03 December 2018